THEM

'I won't serve THEM, ever! And THEY shan't have Petal. I want to join the Prince, so we can get our own back on THEM, ten times over.'

Berlewen and Honesty set off to find the Prince, but a more-than-human danger awaits them on the way. Can they be sure that there really is a Prince – and will the rebellion take the form they are expecting?

Fay Sampson is the author of many books for children, teenagers and adults, including the popular Pangur Bán series. She lives with her husband in a centuries-old cottage overlooking Dartmoor, from which she enjoys walking the moors and coast. As well as writing stories of her own, she loves discovering the story of her ancestors' lives.

TO MATTHEW

Them

FAY SAMPSON

To Debi

best wishes

Fay Sampson.

LION

Text copyright © 2003 Fay Sampson
This edition copyright © 2003 Lion Publishing

The moral rights of the author
have been asserted

Published by
Lion Publishing plc
Mayfield House, 256 Banbury Road,
Oxford OX2 7DH, England
www.lion-publishing.co.uk
ISBN 0 7459 4670 4

First edition 2003
10 9 8 7 6 5 4 3 2 1 0

A catalogue record for this book is available
from the British Library

Typeset in 11/14 Garamond ITC Bk BT
Printed and bound in Great Britain
by Cox and Wyman Ltd, Reading

Chapter One

The drone of the helicopter faded into the distance, leaving only the confused clatter of horses' hooves in the castle yard.

Berlewen St Kew Trethevy hurled herself through the bedroom door and then a muddy riding boot at the chambermaid. The maid side-stepped neatly and shot out her right hand to catch it, while her left arm steered a stack of freshly laundered sheets and pillowslips out of harm's way. Inside her head, Honesty Olds cried Howzat? and heard the storm of applause around the village green. Not, of course, that the fourteen-year-old Countess of Tintagel knew what the chambermaid's name was, still less what went on inside her head.

Honesty still had her hands full when Berlewen threw the other boot. This time she was not quick enough. The heel of the boot struck her on the forehead, leaving a bruise that blossomed crimson and purple, under a thick smear of goose dung.

Honesty's eyes smarted. She gasped, as her laundry toppled down on to the trail of mud left across the floorboards when Berlewen had flung herself on to the pale blue coverlet of the four-poster bed. The maid still held the first boot as she bent to pick up the second.

'Why can THEY have flying machines and cars with engines, and now we can't even ride horses outside the parish?' Berlewen shouted. She was a thundercloud of a girl, with black hair tangled in ringlets, like bladderwrack heaped on the Cornish beach after a storm, and a complexion the purple-red of a poisonous jellyfish. 'THEY're cruel! The only reason THEY make these rules is to show us THEY've got power and we haven't.'

Honesty couldn't help glancing out of the window to convince herself THEIR helicopter had gone. She wisely said nothing. The Countess of Tintagel did not hold conversations with servants. She hurled things at footmen, complaints or boots. They were not expected to throw anything back. And a member of the Trethevy family was not even supposed to *see* a chambermaid.

Berlewen erupted again, but only to turn herself violently on to her stomach and pummel the pillows.

'THEY've made me a prisoner in this piddling parish. I can't hunt on Bodmin Moor now or climb the cliffs at Boscastle or sail to Padstow. What's the use of my father being Grand Duke of Cornwall and the Isles of Scilly, if we can't go further than our own backyard? It doesn't *mean* anything. It's just names.'

It was, of course, THEY who had decided that Berlewen's family should be the aristocrats in a storybook castle, while Honesty's family should be their servants. Real power and terrifying machines belonged only to THEM.

Honesty looked at the filthy boots she was holding and the clean, scattered bedlinen. She couldn't deal with them both at the same time, and her hands were dirty now. She made for the door, bearing the boots, with a backward look of regret at the trail of sheets. It had taken her two hours to iron them.

The bed was bobbing like a boat in a rising wind, as the countess's shoulders in their mustard yellow jacket heaved up and down. Honesty hesitated, then crossed softly to the bedside. Berlewen's square soiled hands were clutching the crumpled coverlet. A dark damp stain was showing beyond her red nose. Honesty shifted both boots to her left hand and bent over. She was two years younger than the Countess of Tintagel, only half the girth, and she would never grow as tall. Her hay-coloured hair fell forward and touched Berlewen's shoulder before her chapped hand did.

'You know what they sing: *One new morning our Prince will appear.*'

It had begun as a whisper, but the snatch of song danced on like a jig.

Berlewen shot up on the bed. 'Who's there? Who are you? What are you doing in my bedroom?' She looked as astonished as if she had stormed into an empty room and the wallpaper had spoken to her.

Honesty's cheeks flamed into horrified embarrassment. She bobbed her head, she bobbed her knees, she clutched the boots and scuttled backwards towards the door, trampling her own footmarks over the sheets and pillowcases.

'I'm sorry! I'm sorry, your grace. I shouldn't have spoken. It won't happen again.'

'You're a what-d'you-me-call-it... maid, aren't you? I'm not supposed to see you.'

Honesty nodded dumbly. The castle rules were clear.

If one of the Family approached the room where you were working, you were supposed to hide in a cupboard or under a table until they were gone. The sheen of the ancient oak furniture, the twinkle of the fireside brasses, the sparkle of the bath on its clawed griffin's paws were supposed to happen as a natural right, not as the result of an army of skivvies getting up at four in the morning to scour and scrub and dust and polish till their elbows ached and their knees grew numb.

'Get out!' snarled Berlewen. She reached for another boot to fling, but the boots and the chambermaid had fled.

Honesty heeled the door to, but quietly, so that it did not quite shut behind her. In her haste to get away, she nearly fell over something like a gigantic rug on the landing outside. It was an untidy heap of shaggy grey hair, with a bright red ridge bristling in a curve from one end to the other.

'Sorry, Prince!' gasped Honesty.

'Sorry,' said the doormat.

An apologetic muzzle extricated itself from a tangle of legs. From under tufted eyebrows two keen yellow eyes gazed up at her. An upheaval at the other end produced a tail like a monkey's, ending in a tassel that resembled frayed rope. A quiver of the haunches set it banging against the floor.

'Hush. I'm in trouble,' said Honesty. And then, 'You'd better go in. I think she needs you.'

While the doormat struggled to its feet, she slipped down the back stairs.

As she turned the bend in the staircase into the shadows below, she almost bumped into someone else. He stepped back against the wall, with a cheerful grin, as though he just happened to be on his way up to the landing she had come from, though there was no reason for the bootboy to be outside the Family bedrooms in the middle of the morning.

All the dirtiest jobs landed on Map. You would find him scrubbing dung off the spokes of carriage wheels, scraping cold grease out of huge iron cauldrons, cleaning the sick off the floor of the Great Hall in the middle of the night, after the duke and his friends had finished a drunken party.

There would be few parties from now on, if THEY stopped people travelling outside their own parish.

She looked at Map questioningly. Under a fall of wavy brown hair, two eyes danced at her. One was brown, the other green. They were disconcerting. He held out his hand.

'Dirty boots? What a good thing I happened to be passing. Allow me.'

Honesty passed them over. The bootboy took them in one hand. His other reached out and gently touched the muddy bruise on her forehead. He licked his finger and wiped the dirt away. The throbbing lump felt cooler.

'*That* bad?'

She nodded. The eyes of both of them went back up the staircase. A sudden thump on the wall made the banisters rattle. The boy's eyes sparkled.

'Temper! Well, her ladyship has her own way of dealing with a bump on the heart.'

He bowed to the chambermaid and waved her down the stairs in front of him, as if she were a lady too. Then he followed her, carrying the dirty boots as ceremoniously as a crown.

Chapter Two

Berlewen hated crying. It made her head ache and her eyes feel as huge and heavy as cannonballs. Her nose ran too.

When her hiccups were coming only once every thirty seconds, she flounced off the high bed, stomped across the floorboards, kicking Honesty's sheets into tangled heaps as she went, and stumbled over her trailing yellow skirt to the door.

The skirt was not the only thing she stumbled over. The door swung violently inwards, almost hitting her on the nose, and a remarkable animal lunged against her legs.

Enkenethals are rare, even in Cornwall. THEY had given orders to exterminate them. Two years ago, the Grand Duke Gwalather's hunt had killed this one's mother on Bodmin Moor. Berlewen had crawled into the beast's lair under the rocks and found an ugly angry pup. To the duke's consternation, she had demanded to take him home with her as a pet, and he had adored her ever since. She called him Petal.

He had grown now to a formidable size, waist-high to Berlewen. His purple snout flared over gums as sharp-toothed as a wolf's, with the same wild yellow eyes and alert ears. The ridge of red hair crested his spine, jagged as a dragon's spikes. His splayed paws showed fearsome talons. His heart was soft as butter. The tasselled tail shivered with anxious enthusiasm.

'Oh, it's you,' she said, balancing on one leg while she rubbed the toe she had stubbed on the in-swinging door. 'Look where you're going.'

The enkenethal lowered milk-blue hoods over his eyes and bent his huge knees until his yellow belly squirmed on the floor. His tail swept the boards nervously.

'Sorry!' he said.

'I suppose you can't help being such a pain, Petal, but I was trying to get out to the garden.'

Petal sprang to his feet, which slid in different directions on the wax-polished floor, so that he banged his chin again.

'Sorry!'

He half padded, half skidded, his way along the gallery after her, like a ragged grey train looped on to the end of her yellow skirt. They clumped down the grand staircase, where only the quiver of a hastily closed door betrayed the presence of terrified housemaids and under-footmen. Then across the black and white tiles of the entrance hall and out into the sunshine of the rose garden.

Berlewen drew her breath in an unintentional gasp. The view was maddeningly beautiful. Over the billowing blossoms of white, pink, crimson and gold roses, an archway of the castle led the eye beyond the cliff top, out to a vista of turquoise sea. It stretched away to the curve of the horizon, blue-green as a duck egg, under a summer sky with only a fluff of white cloud. When she turned her head, the moors behind rose in purple splendour.

Berlewen stamped her foot. 'It's not *fair*. *Why* can't we hunt the wolves on the moor? Why can't we set sail to Lundy Island, or Land's End, or even... *Wales*? THEY have speedboats and fast cars. Why do THEY have to stop us *living*?'

Her stamp grated through the gravel. 'Ouch!' she yelled. She had forgotten her feet were bare.

A pair of riding boots, spotlessly clean and shining with wax, appeared through a clump of hollyhocks beside the path. Berlewen stared at them in astonishment. They were hers, the ones she had thrown at that thingummy – chambermaid? – minutes ago. Framed between them was a boy's face, with a dusting of freckles on his nose. Two eyes stared levelly at her, one green, one brown.

She was not used to seeing a bootboy, still less one who looked her in the eye. It made her feel rather uncomfortable.

Slowly the odd eyes warmed. They started to twinkle. This was even more upsetting.

Remembering that she was the Countess of Tintagel, and that everybody else in Cornwall existed to serve her, Berlewen closed her open mouth and snatched the gleaming boots, without a word of question or thanks. The bent hollyhock stems sprang back into place. The boy's smile vanished.

At the end of the gravel walk, the walls of the kitchen garden rose above her, salmon-red brick, clad in honeysuckle. She shut the gate behind her, almost trapping the enkenethal's tail. The sparkle of the sea and the play of the wind was cut off. It was like crossing the boundary into a different country. Outside on the cliffs, the trees grew sideways, like old people stooping their backs against a gale. Here, peaches ripened against the sun-warmed bricks and butterflies staggered tipsily over the scented herb garden. The windless peace gave it a feeling of privacy.

Berlewen started off down a brick path between rows of fat cabbages and feathery carrot tops. But even here her loss of freedom stung her. The tallest walls could not shut out the heights of the moor, against the sky where buzzards circled.

'I hate THEM!' she shouted. And then even Berlewen St Kew Trethevy clapped her hand over her reckless mouth, in case an informer should hear her.

She glanced round. It was a big garden, but nothing moved in it except the butterflies and a squirrel in the walnut tree.

'Sorry! Sorry!' gulped the enkenethal.

She fondled the ridge between his ears absent-mindedly. 'Don't be stupid, Petal. It's not your fault.'

She trailed more slowly round a corner in the path, her skirt dislodging the perfume of rosemary and thyme. She drove her nails into the palms of her clenched hands in frustration, but they were too blunt to hurt. An irritating snatch of tune went round and round in her head, without getting any further. She flung it into the air, more of an unmusical shout than a song. *'One new morning our Prince will appear…'*

She listened to herself in surprise. She couldn't think

where she had heard it. This wasn't a ballad the minstrels ever sang from the gallery of the Great Hall while the Family dined.

A voice, just as off-key as her own, but deeper, sang back to her, *'And make his land free.'*

Berlewen's heart gave an uncomfortable lurch against her ribs. The shock was both anger and alarm. Surely she still had the right to go where she liked, do whatever she wanted, inside the castle grounds, without being spied on? She was alarmed because whoever had overheard her singing must also have heard her outburst against THEM.

The enkenethal leaped through a row of runner beans in a frenzy of barking. Berlewen followed him over the trampled canes.

She caught the rear view of a large pair of striped trousers, which slowly straightened up to reveal green and yellow braces over a cream smocked shirt, and a large floppy hat like a piece of old sacking. The hat turned, on stiff shoulders, while a knotty hand rubbed the hollow back where the braces met the red and black trousers. There was little to be seen of the face between the droopy hat brim and the vigorous curls of the grey-white beard. But as the neck straightened, the cheeks shone highly polished and as red as the trouser stripes, while the eyes above flashed as blue as the glimpse of the sea outside the walls.

'What are you doing here? You're a… gardener thingummy, aren't you?' Berlewen shouted.

His moustache parted company from his beard, as his mouth fell open in surprise.

'Begging your pardon, miss. I thought you were somebody else.'

'Servants aren't supposed to be where I am. Can't I ever be private?' she raged.

'Ah, well now, maidie. I'm getting a bit old and deaf to be ducking down behind the currant bushes, like we used to have to when I was the garden boy and your dad was a lad.'

The enkenethal had seized his trouser leg with a sound of ripping cloth, but the old man held out his hand to it, palm open. The beast raised apologetic yellow eyes and licked him.

'Sorry!'

'You're not deaf,' Berlewen accused the gardener. 'You sang the next line.'

'Aah.' The earthy hand tipped the hat further back, revealing a shining bald head. The eyes shone very bright and very blue.

'So you did hear me.'

'I heard the song.' The eyes were keener now, as though they held a question.

'Well, I was singing it.'

'I know that *now*. Who taught it to you?'

'I don't remember... Look here! How dare you? Who do you think you are? I'm the Countess of Tintagel. I ask the questions, not some turnip-headed gardener.'

The old man shuffled backwards and touched his hat, shading his eyes again.

'Sorry, my lady. I thought you were somebody else.'

'Sorry!' barked the enkenethal, jumping out of his way.

Berlewen watched in satisfaction as the gardener made a slow and painful retreat behind the potting shed. But the private peace of the garden was spoiled now. Not even a robin, hopping down on to the path beside her to ask if she had uncovered any good worms, could cheer her up.

Notes thrummed in her head, a longer sequence now. She hummed them lower this time.

'La la la-la, la la-la la la,
And make his land free.'

The enkenethal howled along with her.

From over the wall behind her rose a younger voice.

'When the seeds of his kingdom sprout again,
Where will you be?'

Berlewen ran to the gate. Along all the gravel paths and down the terraced flower gardens, there was no one in sight. Only the tall hollyhocks quivered, where the bootboy had stood.

Chapter Three

'THEY might as well shoot the horses,' groaned Gwalather, Grand Duke of Cornwall. 'What's the point of having them, if THEY won't let us hunt?' He flung a pink-stockinged leg over the arm of the dining chair and set the rosette on his blue silk slipper swinging like a pendulum. Under the waxed curl of his black moustache, his lips pouted and he twiddled his black ringlets in irritation.

'Nonsense,' boomed the Grand Duchess Eulalia from the far end of the table. She drew her fine figure up to her full height in her cavalry jacket and adjusted her silver wig. 'One doesn't keep horses to *ride* them. It's for the look of the thing. One needs to show people who the Trethevys are.'

'People? What people?' grumbled her husband. 'If the Grand Duke of Cornwall isn't allowed to ride outside his own parish, what sort of freedom do you suppose the lesser gentry have? We shan't see a soul except the three of us.'

The dining room door swung silently open. A file of soft-shoed footmen glided around the long oak table, removed the soup bowls from Berlewen and her parents and melted, equally silently, back where they had come from. Footmen, of course, were not people.

'Why?' burst out Berlewen. 'Why can't we go where we want?'

Her father tapped the side of his nose with a knowing, sideways look. 'If you ask me, my dear, THEY are afraid of us. The aristocracy, you know. It's in the blood. Ruling people. Been doing it since the Flood, our lot. And THEY're just jumped up nobodies. No pedigree at all. Stands to reason THEY're scared of the real thing.'

'Careful, my dear.' The Grand Duchess shot a look at the door where the servants had disappeared.

'But why should THEY be scared? What could we do, against THEM?' Berlewen asked.

'Do?' bellowed her mother, from the far end of the table. 'The aristocracy don't do things, you silly child. We just *are*. We leave *doing* things to little people, who work for a living. Like dairymaids, gamekeepers, kings. That sort of common people.'

'Are kings common?'

'I should think so,' said her father, combing his fingers through his curls. 'Always have to be busy with something. Making laws. Leading battles. Opening garden parties. Devil of a life, if you ask me.'

'How do you know that? We haven't got a king. Did we have one once? Before THEM?'

The door swung open again and the train of seven footmen bore aloft on silver salvers a roast swan, a boar's head, a haunch of venison, a stuffed salmon, a Peking duck and a bowl of plum sauce. The smallest of them carried the gravy.

'Aah,' said the Grand Duke Gwalather, spearing the

apple stuffed into the boar's mouth and waving the meat away.

Berlewen felt her question trickling away into emptiness, as it always did when she asked about the time before THEM.

The Grand Duchess Eulalia fixed her eyes on the row of platters and motioned to the butler to keep carving until her plate was piled chin-high. A ladleful of plum sauce slithered over it to cascade stickily across the polished table. She seized her dagger and fork.

An unfamiliar noise droned up the drive and stopped. The bell clanged through the echoes of the entrance hall.

The first footman had just reached Berlewen. The dead swan's beak dropped over the edge of the platter and tapped her shoulder, as everyone froze.

'Visitors?' said the duke. 'At the front door?' He sounded nervous.

'They weren't riding horses,' said Berlewen. 'That was a *machine*.'

The temperature in the dining room seemed to drop to a wintry chill. Only THEY were permitted to use engines.

The butler moved swiftly into the entrance hall, through a grander door than the one to the kitchen. The Grand Duke's eyes were on it. The silent footmen looked at each other and glided back against the walls.

Berlewen kept her back to that door and beckoned to the footman with the Peking duck. She was not going to show her curiosity or her fear. Now that she had been stopped from riding the moor and sailing, nothing nice could happen, and probably never would again. No matter how rich she was, or how many titles she had,

THEY would not allow her to go anywhere, do anything, meet other people. THEY had just taken away even the little freedom she had had. She was only fourteen and her life was over.

There was a cry from beyond the door, a clang of metal, a thud, then a prolonged wail, growing fainter, as if the butler had hit the floor and was slithering away into the distance. Another bump, then silence. The door from the entrance hall flew open.

'Sorry your butler couldn't announce us, darlings. He seems to have lost his voice.' An immensely tall young man, with huge shoulders and a broad bare chest, slouched into the room. He wore a black leather waistcoat, hung about with iron chains, and camouflage trousers tucked into studded boots. His knuckles were studded too, clenched ostentatiously just outside his pockets. An orange crest of hair ran across his shaved scalp. Behind him came another young man, almost as tall but cadaverously thin, in an elegant chalk-striped suit tailored to every hollow of his body. A purple streak ran oddly through his carefully cut black hair. The eyes of both sparkled with a cold laughter.

'Now which of you would be…' The thin young man in the suit drew a folded paper from the inside pocket of his jacket. He read, with a mocking flourish, 'Berlewen… Zenobia… St Kew… Trethevy… Countess of Tintagel?'

Orange-Top spluttered with suppressed laughter.

The tiny push Berlewen gave her chair made an enormous screech on the bare floor.

'I am.'

'Hello, darling. I hoped it was you, not that sandbag in corsets with the big appetite. Is that your old woman?' The big stranger in the leather waistcoat sauntered down the table, picked up the Grand Duchess's dinner plate and tilted it over her head. A single drop of plum sauce trickled down the stiffly clenched outrage of her face.

'Gwalather! *Do* something!'

'What do you suggest, my dear? I'm a Grand Duke, not a prize wrestler. And they've got one of those gun… things.'

Berlewen's eyes had been drawn in fascination to the unfamiliar weapon at Orange-Top's hip.

'Have these… scum… thrown out.'

Six platters of six footmen shivered. No one made eye contact. The intruder in the suit leaned over Berlewen's shoulder and lifted the leg of duck from her plate. His teeth picked at it fastidiously.

'Not bad. A little too much ginger.'

'I'm afraid,' Gwalather said to his wife, 'the butler is unavailable to show them the door.'

Orange-Top fondled the Grand Duke's ear with a greasy hand. 'That's it, pop. You're getting the idea. We weren't planning to stop long, as it happens. We just want the girl.'

'Gwalather!'

Berlewen went ice cold. The men were on either side of her, looking down, laughing, too near.

'I do believe,' grinned the one with the orange crest, 'she thinks we fancy her.'

The slimmer man put the chewed duck bone back on her plate. His other hand came round and waved the folded sheet of paper in front of her eyes. She grew dizzy watching it.

'Oh, no, madam. We wouldn't dare touch *you*. Not unless you were *very* naughty. No. There's plans higher up for you. THEY want you... *Now*!'

He dropped the folded document, bound with black ribbon, alongside her plate. But as he drew his hand away, it strayed up under her chin, thumb splayed, fingers stretched, testing his grip lightly around her throat. Though his hand did not tighten, Berlewen choked.

There was a volcanic upheaval under the dining table. Plates of food sprang into the air as the enkenethal erupted from his slumber on Berlewen's feet. Like a torrent of grey lava streaked with red, his enormous body poured forth so fast he seemed to occupy ten times his normal space. He struck the long thin messenger in the suit so hard that the man toppled horizontally and skidded across the floor, to ram his head into the doorpost like a battering ram. Orange-Top snatched a gun from the bulge on his hip.

'Petal!' shrieked Berlewen. 'Down!'

Enkenethal and thug circled around the prostrate Purple-Streak, who lay pale and blank-eyed, staring up. Both man and beast on their feet had their teeth bared, muscles bunched, and breathed in panting growls. Orange-Top's gun flashed. There was a deafening bang. Splinters flew from the oak panelling over the smallest footman's head.

A violent curse broke from the thug. 'This thing's fired wide again!'

The enkenethal's talons scraped the floor. As Petal hurled himself at Orange-Top's chest, the gun went spinning across the floor. The man lunged after it, then seeing it out of reach, grabbed for his knife. He was braced to hold himself against Petal's weight. The biceps on his naked arm stood out, tensed to aim the blade steady at the enkenethal's throat. There was a quiver of bristling grey hair, a scratching of claws on oak. A growl rumbled in Petal's chest.

The prostrate man in the suit rolled over. His hand gripped the enkenethal's fore paw. With a violent heave, he sent the astonished beast whirling over his head and launched him like a rock from a catapult, hurtling across the hall.

'Scarper!' yelled his sidekick. 'That brute's a killer!'

Purple-Streak was on his knees, to his feet, long legs in striped trousers streaking for the front door before the enkenethal could recover. Orange-Top grabbed up the gun, fired wildly and pounded after him. There was a roar as the four-wheel-drive vehicle bucked round on the drive, spitting sheets of gravel, and aimed its bullbars at the gate.

There was an echoing roar from the hall. The enkenethal howled.

'Petal!' Berlewen raced from the dining room. 'Are you all right?'

Petal shook his monstrous head. His teeth rattled and several fell out on the floor. There was blood on the torn corners of his gums. He raised his mournful yellow eyes to her. Then his ears stiffened. His head turned. As the vehicle's engine crashed into forward gear, the enkenethal hurled himself across the rose garden in frantic pursuit.

'Petal! No! It's all right. They've gone.' Berlewen tried to whistle, but no sound would come. Petal was already scorching through the gates, his tail twanging the wrought iron bars.

'It's not all right,' called Berlewen's mother's deep voice. 'You've had THEIR summons.'

There were two loud reports.

Berlewen was leaping down the steps. She skidded to a stop. That was the sound the gun had made. What could these gun-things do to you, if they fired straight? Her eyes strained after two dust clouds. The enkenethal seemed to be falling behind the vehicle as it progressed erratically over the bumpy road. Loyal, foolish Petal. What hope did he have, anyway, of catching up with the machines of THEM?

Her ears were tuned to her mother's voice now. Of course, THEIR letter. She felt the cold sinking of her heart into a bottomless well.

Slowly she walked back to the dining room. She was aware of the stiffening of her cheek muscles, which told her she had gone pale. As soon as she reached the inner doorway she saw the document still lying on the table, where Purple-Streak had dropped it. A triple fold of creamy parchment, tied with black ribbon. She did not want to look at it. Treacherously, she felt more sick than when she had seen the gun aimed at Petal's jugular, and hated herself for her smallness of spirit. That was not noble.

THEY had this effect on people. It seemed that nothing you could do, nothing you could dare, nothing you could even hope for, would ever get you out from under the vast grey weight of power, which was crushing life from the country. THEY made you smaller, THEY made you meaner, because you could no longer even dream of becoming anything more.

Her father was sitting, foolishly holding his dagger and fork, which rattled against the table as his hands trembled. The Grand Duchess was standing, her corseted chest heaving, but her face sternly under control, scornful of the streak of plum sauce.

Berlewen did not want to cross the space to the table and pick up the letter.

'Aren't you going to tell us what it says?' asked her mother.

Berlewen wanted more than anything to bury her face in the rough hairs of the enkenethal's neck. Where was he? Why hadn't he come back? A voice in her head, which sounded unreal and far away, was telling her she was a Trethevy, the Countess of Tintagel, and she must walk across the room bravely and read that letter. Her body was telling her she was scared stiff.

That gunshot couldn't have hit Petal, could it? Surely he couldn't still be pursuing THEIR vehicle half across Cornwall? She had seen the gap between those dust clouds widening, as though the enkenethal's energy was failing. She had a sudden terrible vision of disaster. What if his brave heart had burst and he was lying dead on the stony road? She should never have turned back from the gate. She must run and find him. Now!

That would mean turning her back on THEIR letter. It was a command from THEM. She had to obey. Only a crazy orphaned savage enkenethal would think that love and loyalty mattered more than power, and that love could change things.

Her movements were slow, as though iron balls were

chained to her ankles. Her parents waited. Too soon, she reached the table and stood staring down. A spatter of gravy had stained the pristine parchment. It brought the faintest smile to Berlewen's face. It was only a tiny disrespect. Nothing as awful as Petal flattening THEIR messenger... She closed her mind swiftly on the possible consequences of that. But her eyes went to the tall windows.

'Petal! Petal!' she agonized silently.

While her thoughts had been distracted, she found she had picked up the letter. It was cool, stiff, heavier than ordinary paper. Her fingers were incapable of managing the knots in the black ribbon. She shuffled it off. At first, the words were only a dance of black pen strokes, then a nonsense chant of syllables in her head. Slowly her brain marshalled them into sense.

'Well?' said her father, almost a sob.

'I have to report to Headquarters. Immediately. No one is to accompany me, except the escort provided. I am to take no personal possessions. The Supreme Council for Justice and Peace will provide everything necessary. "You have been selected from thousands of your age group for the highest honour of dedicating your life to the service of your beloved Fatherland. Congratulations."'

She dropped the document and looked again out of the window, to the gorse bushes vivid gold on the cliff edge, to the turquoise and jade sea of the shallow bay where fishing smacks bobbed, to the breeze rippling the silvery meadows that were ripening to hay. Was this the Fatherland? Cornwall? She would dedicate her life to it, wouldn't she? But Headquarters was hundreds of miles upcountry. She was sure that love like this was not what THEY meant.

She felt again Purple-Streak's fingers round her throat, saw Orange-Top draw his gun to kill Petal. Had they once been ordinary boys? Had they had letters like hers, summoning them to Headquarters?

'You'll have to go,' said the Grand Duchess, in a strained, proud voice. 'You can't refuse the Supreme Council. And the Trethevys have always served their country. Of course, I mean Cornwall.'

'She can't go.' Her father's voice was flat with gloom, like the sluggish swell in the shadow of a breakwater. 'Her enkenethal attacked THEIR escort. They've gone to report her.'

The enormity of what had just happened silenced them all. Even a joke against the Supreme Council was treason to the Fatherland. There could be no opposition. And Berlewen's Petal had thrown himself savagely on THEIR messengers.

'They'll be back.' The Grand Duke's voice trembled.

'What will they do to him?' Berlewen's own voice was not steady either.

Nobody answered. There was a little whistle from the smallest footman. Berlewen looked up sharply. His head was bent, but there was something familiar about the sparkle of gold freckles on his nose and a smudge of bootblack on his cheek.

All this time the other six footmen had been standing frozen against the wall, like so many white-faced pillars. Now the Grand Duke snapped his fingers at them and they sprang to life, as if released from hypnotic trance. One of them even began to spoon salmon on to

Berlewen's plate. Gwalather waved him back impatiently.

'Girl's not hungry, idiot! Take it away.'

With impassive dignity, the servants carried the remains of the family luncheon through the door to the kitchen. Berlewen, almost in a trance herself, wandered out through the opposite door into the hall. The butler, cursing horribly, was scrambling to his knees, helped now by the smallest footman. On the side of his head, he had a lump the size of a goose egg, only dark blue. He tried to draw himself up into a position from which he could bow, but fell over again. The little footman darted forward to catch him in surprisingly strong arms.

Berlewen walked past, without speaking to either of them.

Chapter Four

She stood on the drive and whistled again, producing a thin, if hopeless, sound this time. The enkenethal did not come.

'Petal! Petal! Here, boy!' The wind carried her words back from the cliff.

'THEY wouldn't have let me take him to Headquarters, anyway.'

The words, spoken aloud, frightened her. If she went to Headquarters, she would not come back. Her childhood was over, but she would never be Duchess of Cornwall now in her father's place. THEY would claim her.

But what would THEY do to her now?

'Nothing good is ever going to happen to me again.'

The snatch of a song floated through her mind. *One new morning our Prince will appear...*

'What prince?' she said aloud, angrily. 'There's only THEM.'

She broke into a run, down the sweeping drive to the gate. The road was empty. She ran along it. The thick dust was impressed with the strangely patterned marks of the vehicle's tyres. A carriage without horses, the kind of power only THEY were allowed to use. So loud, so fast, so strong. There were paw-prints too, far apart, where Petal had chased after the intruders in huge bounds.

'Oh, Pet, why did you do it?'

His leaps had become shorter. She was flagging herself now. Then she pulled up suddenly. There were dark spatters in the dust. She had been hunting for too many years not to know at once what they were. Blood, still fresh.

'Petal?'

Then, nothing. The vehicle tracks went on. The paw marks and the bloodstains ended. She scanned the grass on either side of the road. There was no sign of the enkenethal, dead or alive.

'Petal,' she wailed. 'Did they get you?'

In a blur of tears she trailed back to the house. She did not want to go inside and face her parents. She walked round the corner of the house, kicking the gravel.

'I hate THEM.'

There was no Petal bounding at her heels. There never would be again. She could not bear it.

She was not sure why she opened the gate into the walled garden, but she felt that there was a reason nagging at the back of her mind. As the latch closed behind her, she was aware of the warm stillness of the air trapped between old brickwork. She scanned the paths between the beds and knew with a shock what she was looking for. She wanted the gardener.

It was an astonishing thought. Servants were only to be seen if absolutely necessary. They did what you

31

ordered and disappeared as silently as possible into parts of the house you need never see. They did not stand their ground and call you 'maidie' and look at you with bright, intelligent eyes. They did not leave you feeling they knew much more than they had told you.

She had hummed the first line of the song she had got from the chambermaid and the gardener had sung her the next. *'And make his land free.'*

What did it mean?

It doesn't have to mean anything. It's just some old peasants' pub song.

But she wanted it to mean more than that.

She sang the first line quite loudly and stopped. The bees hummed over the lavender. She walked on between the asparagus beds, her boots clicking on the brick path, and sang the second line. A far more musical blackbird challenged her from the cherry tree. There was no one else in the garden.

She turned to face the wall behind her. What were the lines that had come over it, from someone outside?

'When the seeds of his kingdom sprout again,
Where will you be?'

The bootboy? Oh, this was ridiculous.

All this time, her ears were strained for a different sound from outside, the sound that must surely come. The roar of an armoured vehicle, the drone of a helicopter in the sky, the whine of a powerboat cutting in towards the harbour, any of the machines only THEY were allowed to use. They would surely come, after what Petal had done. How much time did she have left?

At the far end, the garden began to climb towards the moor. Through a wrought iron gate she caught a glimpse of short turf, bushes of gorse, the silhouettes of windswept hawthorn trees. A line of sheets was flapping in the breeze.

The moor spoke to her of a last look at freedom. She went towards it.

The gate clanged behind her. Her boots rang against rock. From the other side of the billowing sheets a girl's voice sang. *'One new morning our Prince will appear.'*

Berlewen's gruff voice responded. *'And make his land free.'*

A thin astonished face popped through the curtains of wet white linen.

'I beg your pardon, my lady!' The maid broke off in horror when she saw Berlewen, Countess of Tintagel. Colour flamed under her freckles. 'I thought...' She disappeared behind the sheets again. The laundry basket was snatched up out of sight.

'Wait!' Berlewen forced her way through the flapping folds. The girl was small and skinny, with hay-coloured hair. 'Who are you?'

'Honesty Olds.' The girl bobbed a curtsey. 'Chambermaid, ma'am.'

Something snagged at the back of Berlewen's mind. 'Haven't I seen you before?'

'Yes'm. I... I'd come to change the sheets on your bed, when I thought you'd gone... hunting.' The last word whispered.

'THEY forbade us to leave the parish. And you were in the way when I threw my boot and... It was *you* taught me the song!'

The girl pressed her lips together. She looked terrified.

33

'I shouldn't have done it. It's just a song we sing. It doesn't mean anything.'

'Then why did you sing it back to me, when you heard me coming? As if it was… a password?'

The girl's eyelids dropped. 'I made a mistake. Coming from the garden… I thought it must be Grandad.'

'And what would your grandfather be doing in the gardens of Trethevy Castle?'

'He's the gardener, my lady.'

A picture blossomed in Berlewen's mind of a round rear in red and black trousers, a slowly straightening back, a pair of bright blue eyes.

'He taught me the second line.'

'*Did* he?' Honesty swiftly raised her eyes. She looked impressed. She came forward, parting the wet washing. Her gaze was level now, like her grandfather's, not dropping humbly before the countess's stare. 'Then he must have thought you…' Her eyes widened with shock. They went past Berlewen, to the pale blue sky above the sea, where a hum like a gnat was swelling to a drone.

'THEY're coming back, my lady.'

Berlewen whipped round. The helicopter was no more than a small black fly yet, but it was powering towards them.

'Those thugs again! Oh, Petal, why did you do it? Where *are* you?'

'I heard they fired… guns.'

A flush darkened Berlewen's cheeks. 'I'd never seen one go off before. It made a lot of noise, but it didn't hurt anybody. I'm not sure what all the fuss is about.'

Honesty frowned. 'There's something wrong, then.

They don't usually miss.' She raised her hands and took a sight along an imaginary weapon. 'Bang! And then you're dead. Even if you're as far away as that tree.'

Berlewen clapped her hand to her mouth. 'Petal? There was blood on the road. What if they hit him, after all! They wouldn't, would they?... Oh, yes, they would! I hate them! Oh, Petal!'

'And now they're coming back for you, my lady.'

'I won't go! I'll throw myself off the cliff rather than serve THEM. If they've killed Petal...'

'He was a one, wasn't he? Knocking him over like that? Everyone's talking about it below stairs, my lady. Map told us all about it.' Honesty looked round at the sea, the castle, the moorland behind her, a little wildly. 'But they're not just going to take you to serve THEM now, ma'am. It'll be worse than that, after what he did. But it's not going to help, you throwing yourself off the cliff, is it? Let me think.'

'*You?*'

Just for a moment, a look of anger crossed the chambermaid's face, as though she was thinking of saying, 'All right, then. Suit yourself.' Honesty controlled herself. She spoke with rapid emphasis, as if she had leaped to a decision she did not have time to weigh.

'Listen, my lady. There's something else you could do. There is a Prince. Grandad believes so, anyway, and so do I. He says before THEY took over, it wasn't like this. There was a king at the palace – a bit like THEIR Headquarters, but in London – and everyone wanted to serve him, because he always did what was best for the land. Grandad says it felt like one big family, working together, with the king at the head, like a father.'

'Like my father, the Grand Duke?'

'Well…' Honesty hesitated diplomatically, 'not *exactly*.'

The drone was growing louder.

'But the king's gone. That was before Father was born. What about me, now?'

Honesty brought her face close to Berlewen's and whispered. 'But he's *not* gone. He left a son. Now there's always a Prince in waiting. That's why we sing the song to each other, so we keep on hoping. Somewhere still, there's a Prince in hiding. And we're like his…' she turned pink, 'secret agents. We've got to stay loyal, we've got to be ready, for when he comes.'

The helicopter was clearly visible, skimming the cliffs, less than two miles away, sinister as a bluebottle.

Berlewen gripped the maid's arm. 'Where is he? I'm going to find him and join his army! I'll beat the living daylights out of THEM for Petal. We'll ride back here with banners flying and the Prince at our head. We'll free Cornwall from THEM.'

Just for a moment, Honesty's face glowed with enthusiasm too, as though a lamp had been lit under her freckled skin. Then her expression fell. She was a twelve-year-old chambermaid, nervously shuffling her feet in the dusty grass. 'I don't know, my lady. Nobody knows where the Prince is. Not even Grandad.'

The nearing beat of the helicopter's blades was drumming fear into Berlewen's veins. 'If they catch me now, I'll never find him. They're almost here!' Her glance flew over the rising moorland, the garden behind her open to the sky. 'And there's nowhere to hide.'

'There is, my lady. If you're quick.'

Honesty dropped the basket and the last of the sheets

tumbled out in the sun. She seized Berlewen's bigger hand in her own. They started to run.

There was a massive gorse bush in the way, a prickly stockade of green spikes, scattered with gold. Honesty seemed to be racing straight into it. At the last moment, Berlewen tried to pull her away and dodge around it, but the chambermaid pushed her to the ground, quite roughly. Berlewen fell on her knees and saw a tunnel under the arching sprays of furze. As Honesty shoved her from behind, she scrambled forward.

There was a hollow at the centre of the thicket. Thin grass, peaty soil, groping roots. Through the branches of gorse, a circle of sky still showed clear above. The helicopter's engine became very loud.

'Down there!'

Under the chambermaid's push, the countess's face almost hit the ground. What Berlewen had taken to be a deep shadow beneath the tallest bushes was a cleft in the earth. They both threw themselves into it, as the machine passed overhead. A moment later the rotors clattered to a halt.

'They've landed.'

As the engine died, they listened to the sound of their own panting. Then there were shouted orders. A quick succession of bangs.

'Are those… guns? Ones that can fire straight?'

Honesty nodded. 'I'm afraid so.'

'My… Ow!' Berlewen had tried to scramble upright and hit her head on the roof of roots. 'My parents! They'll shoot them instead, if they can't find me. I've got to go back!'

Honesty hung on to her. 'I don't *think* they will.

Grandad said… begging your pardon, my lady… THEY think it's a good idea to have dukes and duchesses and such, with castles and horses and coaches. Like in children's storybooks. So people will feel happy and won't bother about what THEY're doing. THEY'd never allow a king, of course, and the dukes don't have any real power. So perhaps THEY won't want to kill the Grand Duke and Duchess…' She ducked involuntarily, as another quick volley of firing was followed by a deeper '*crump*'. 'Only they might be knocking the castle about a bit.'

'You don't know that.' Berlewen bit her lip. 'You're only guessing.'

Honesty went pale as the gunfire continued. 'It's too late now, anyway. Somebody's getting it. You can't go back, my lady. It wouldn't do any good.'

Berlewen slumped beside her. There wasn't room to straighten her neck. She stared at the shadowed earth at her feet.

There was an odd smell. Berlewen's nose wrinkled as she drew in a deep breath of it. There was something familiar about it, like old socks and wet wool and a pheasant carcase that has been hung to ripen just too long. Her throat choked.

'Petal! It's his smell.'

Crouched in the near darkness of the burrow, Honesty's voice came muffled. 'Your enkenethal used to come here. I'd cadge a bone, if I could, off the cooks. He needed somewhere private to take it.' She nudged something against Berlewen's hand. It was a short shank, knobbed at one end and gnawed into blunt splinters at the other. 'He loved it when there was marrow inside.'

'Petal? Those times he wouldn't come, no matter how hard I whistled? That was you? How dare you! He's my pet!'

'Shh!'

'Don't you shush me!' Berlewen raged, though in a quieter hiss.

They huddled together. Their hiding place was too narrow for them to draw apart. The guns had fallen silent. Occasional voices shouted.

'Do you think they're searching for me?'

'Probably.'

Berlewen cradled the bone against her cheek.

'Petal's dead. They shot him.'

Summoning her courage, the chambermaid brushed the countess's hand. 'He'll make us free one day. The Prince.' She hummed the last lines of the song.

'When the seeds of his kingdom sprout again,
Where will you be?'

Chapter Five

Outside the burrow light drained from the sky. Pain scorched the girls' cramped muscles when they tried to move. There was no room to change position. Each stirring of the air woke the rank smell of the enkenethal. Berlewen tried to remain numb, not moving, not feeling. Her first flash of courage had died. She did not want to leave this burrow ever again and face the world without Petal.

Suddenly Honesty gasped, 'Shh!' though both girls had been silent for hours.

There were voices approaching, harsh shouting, feet making the hard ground quiver. Brushwood snapped at the smash of sticks. Berlewen grabbed Honesty's hand, excusing herself that the younger girl might be frightened. There was nowhere to run. A merciless blue-white light cut the twilight, colder than any lantern flame. Diamond points pierced the black thicket of gorse.

The light travelled across the space outside the burrow. The girls held their breath. The edge of the beam passed over the grass and left it in deep shadow. The shouting receded.

Berlewen was just opening her mouth to say, 'They've gone,' when there was the crack of dry twigs from the other side of the bushes. It was more furtive, more sinister than the glare of electric searchlights, the thrashing batons, the bullying voices. There was no picture in their minds, no name for what was shuffling towards them. The girls' eyes widened in the dark. This noise did not pass by. The rustle and scratch of breaking spines grew more persistent. Whatever it was, it was forcing its way in. Berlewen made out the gorse hedge shaking against the last grey in the sky above the sea. She heard the snuffle of heavy breath.

'Oh!' A tiny bubble of sound popped out of Honesty's mouth before she could catch it back. Berlewen's fingers crushed her hand. The sky was emptied of light, as a huge body blanked out the first misty stars. Out of the darkness there was a blaze of yellow eyes. The beast flung itself across the open hollow, teeth gaping in a momentary gleam. The force of bristling hair, powering bone, raking claws, flying slobber, hit the mouth of the burrow and came crashing in on them. A wild wet tongue slapped Berlewen's face. The stench rose tenfold.

Honesty flung her arms around its neck. 'Prince!'

'Petal!' gasped the smothered voice of Berlewen from underneath him.

'Sorry! Sorry! Sorry!' mumbled the enkenethal in ecstatic pants.

'Get off!' gasped Berlewen.

With the difficulty of ungainly legs and hurt feelings, the enkenethal backed out again into the circle of gorse. The girls crawled after him.

'Shh!' whispered Honesty, half laughing, half terrified. 'They're not far away.'

'There's something caught in his teeth.' Berlewen disengaged from his muzzle a scrap of soggy leather. Under the slime she felt two metal studs. It was very like what she had seen on the waistcoat of the orange-haired thug.

'Petal! What did you do to them?'

Honesty had been fondling his ears. Suddenly the enkenethal leaped backwards with a howl. She went down on her knees to him, reaching out more gently. Her fingers came away sticky too, but not with slobber. 'Miss, feel this. Careful, though.'

Petal whined as Berlewen found the wound. Part of his ear had been torn away and a gouge scored across the side of his skull, stripping the hair. Blood had crusted in clots, stemming the flow, but at the slight movement of the girls' hands it was oozing again.

'Is this what guns do?' asked Berlewen.

'*Much* worse than that, from what Grandad says. He was lucky. I bet it hurts, though. Poor Prince!'

Fear silenced them, in spite of their joy, so there was only the enkenethal's noisy breathing. Guns belonged to a different world, with electricity and internal combustion engines and flying machines and instruments that let you talk to somebody far away. They were the tools of THEM. What could ordinary people do against THEM, without these things?

'*What* did you call him?' demanded Berlewen after a while.

'P-prince.' Honesty's voice quavered.

'His name's Petal.

'I know, miss. But, well, he seems like a prince…
to me.'

'He's *my* pet. Not yours. *I* saved him from the moor.
I named him.'

'I know, my lady. I'm sorry, my lady.'

'Sorry! Sorry!' agreed the enkenethal.

Berlewen glared at both of them, though she could
not see Honesty now, and only the glow of Petal's yellow
eyes.

'Now you'll both have to escape,' said Honesty. 'And
you'd better hurry, as soon as that lot have gone.'

'Where can I go?'

'Come on.'

Honesty was already on her hands and knees,
crawling out of the tunnel through the gorse. Berlewen
tried to follow, but Petal got in the way. She let him
scrabble ahead of her, waiting until clods of earth had
ceased to fly.

There was more light out in the open, above the
castle gardens. It was still possible to make out the
layers of sky and sea and land. Stabs of light zigzagged
viciously over the hillside to their right. More lights
glared in the castle windows, totally unlike the soft glow
of candles. Berlewen tried not to let herself wonder
what had happened to her father and mother.

Honesty set off to the left, away from the castle.

The line of washing gleamed faintly in the gloom. The
chambermaid stopped. Right at the end of the line, past
the big squares of sheets and the small rectangles of
pillowslips, which she had had to wash a second time,
hung something slighter. She quickly unpegged it and
held it out to the countess.

43

'It'll be a bit tight, my lady, though Mum cut it on the big side, for when I grow. But it'll be safer than that gold velvet, if anyone stops us.'

Berlewen's hand reached for the gingham dress as distastefully as she would for a half-chewed bone of the enkenethal's. Still, she saw the sense of it. She stripped off her riding habit. It was a fight to get the frock on over her bulkier figure.

'Couldn't I have a boy's breeches and one of those smock things?' she complained from inside the folds.

'It's all I've got,' said Honesty firmly. 'And my brothers are smaller than me... At least...' Her voice wavered.

She recovered herself and retrieved the rest of the washing. They carried the heavy basket between them.

'I'm sorry, my lady. It's just in case we meet anybody.'

'In the middle of the night?'

'You're right. It's after curfew. We'd better hurry.'

There was candlelight in the cottage in the hollow, soft, golden. Honesty set down the basket and went ahead, opening the door cautiously.

In a few moments she was back.

'It's all right. Those thugs were here, but they've gone now.'

The small cottage seemed full of people. Berlewen recognized Honesty's grandfather first, in spite of the huge red and purple bruise across his face. The blow had split the skin on his cheekbone. There was a woman who must be Honesty's mother, though she was twice her size. She had bald red patches on her scalp, where handfuls of her hair seemed to have been torn out. An assortment of small, scared boys and girls gathered

44

round the scrubbed table, staring at the Countess of Tintagel in their sister's gingham dress.

As Honesty finished their story, Grandfather whistled, the tune now familiar. 'So, maidie,' he winked, 'you've decided it's time to take sides?'

Berlewen bit back the impulse to be outraged that a gardener should address her like that. It was harder to feel like a countess in a servant's too-small dress. Oddly enough, this old man seemed to have more authority than her father, even with the angry wound across his face.

'What's happened at the castle? How are my parents?'

The deep blue eyes softened. He paused. 'Never you fear. They're as well as I am.' His hand strayed to his wound. He winced as he raised his arm. 'THEIR sort don't question gently. But they left your folks alive.'

'I was afraid... if THEY were trying to find where I was... Of course, my parents didn't know... but still...'

'They tied them up and then they shot the horses. In front of them,' piped up the youngest boy.

'Hush, Nick! You didn't have to tell her that,' scolded his mother.

'All the horses? Even my pony? No!' Berlewen screamed.

'When they lined us all up against the wall, I thought they were going to shoot the servants, one by one, if the old duke didn't talk,' said Grandfather. 'But they must have reckoned your daddy cared more about his horses than he did about us.'

Berlewen bit her lip.

'I see you got your enkenethal back, then.'

'He bit one of them. And they shot him. Look at his head.'

'Aah. He's a grand fool.'

'We've got to get away now, both of us. I won't serve THEM, ever! And THEY shan't have Petal. I want to join the Prince, so we can get our own back on THEM, ten times over.'

'Do you, now, maidie?' He looked her over steadily. 'And where do you reckon on finding this Prince, since nobody else can?'

'I thought you knew.'

'We sing the Prince's song. We keep ourselves ready for his coming. But none of us knows where he is.'

'Haven't you even got a clue? You must know *something*. How else could his song have started?'

'Well... come close.' He drew her over to the side of the room. The space was too small to be out of earshot of the children, so he bent his mouth to her ear and murmured, 'There are rebels gathering. And they do say, the day they strike for freedom, the Prince will come back to lead his own.'

'Rebels!' gasped Berlewen too loudly. 'Where?'

Grandfather clapped an earthy-smelling hand over her mouth. 'Shh! It won't be as easy to reach them as you think. But if I were you, I'd make for...' he touched the side of his nose and whispered again.

'Gla...?'

'*Silence*!' he thundered, so that everyone flinched. 'Can't you keep a secret? Do you want to put their lives in danger?' He was looking at the little ones.

'How do I get to... this island?'

The old man nodded at Honesty. 'I'll see she knows. And how to tell a safe house, if you should pass by one.'

Berlewen looked round. Honesty looked different,

taller. She had changed into a pair of boy's trousers, tied with string. Over a baggy smock she wore a dark jacket.

'Are you coming too?' Berlewen asked. 'There's going to be fighting, you know.'

As Honesty scowled, Grandfather chuckled, 'I doubt you'd get far without her.'

'Why can't I have trousers?' Berlewen objected. 'Those look big enough. You said...'

'These were my brother Colan's. He's... not with us.'

There was a muffled sound from her mother. Honesty went to her and hugged her hard. All the children were holding up their arms to their sister. She tried to hum the Prince's tune and failed.

'Take my winter cloak,' said her mother, holding it out to Berlewen. 'It's got a good deep hood. I wish I could make you up a proper packet of food, but they've robbed us of almost everything.'

She put a heel of dry bread and a rind of cheese in a knapsack. Grandfather went out to rummage through the hay in the shed and came back with a small dusty flagon of cider. The enkenethal made his own investigation of the compost heap and proudly extricated a rather smelly fish head.

As the girls crossed the threshold, a figure moved in the starlight. The girls froze in alarm. Someone jumped down off the pigpen where he had been perching and strolled towards them.

'Going somewhere?'

'Map!' Honesty breathed in relief. 'The bootboy,' she explained to Berlewen. 'He's my best friend.'

The light was too dim for Berlewen to see those odd eyes, one brown, one green. But she could tell from the chuckle in his voice that those eyes must be dancing.

'I'm going to find the Prince and fight for him,' declared Berlewen, 'if it's the last thing I do.'

'We're going to...' Honesty stood on tiptoe and whispered in his ear.

'*That* far?'

'Well, we won't find the Prince by staying here, will we?' said Berlewen belligerently.

'No?' Again the laughter quivered in Map's voice.

'My father's the Grand Duke. If the Prince was anywhere in Cornwall, we'd know about it.'

There was a long unsettling silence.

'Well, if you're sure about that, you'll be needing these.' The starlight glinted on two stout staffs. Map handed one to each girl. He held Honesty's shoulders and kissed her warmly.

'Go well, friend.'

His hands closed round Berlewen's as she took his staff.

'Come back safely... your ladyship!'

She caught her breath as he planted a firm kiss on her cheek. Then the bootboy stepped away from her into the shadows and was gone.

It was several moments before Berlewen recovered from her astonishment. Even in the silence outside the cottage, she was careful now. 'How long will it take us to get to...' her voice dropped, 'Glastonbury?'

'Weeks, if we have to walk it, and only travel in the dark.'

'And you really think nobody is going to notice we've got an enkenethal with us and betray us to THEM?'

'We mustn't let ourselves be seen. Do you want to go back?'

Berlewen looked over her shoulder. The castle was still lit with those strange harsh lights. 'No.'

A little later. 'Do you think the Prince is really there? On that island?'

'There's no one can say the answer to that. The song sounds a bit as if we have to start the rising, and then he'll come. We won't know until we get there. As long as we can get across…'

'Across what?'

But Honesty would say no more.

She led Berlewen up the moorland path that would take them out of Cornwall.

Chapter Six

Long before they reached the city, they saw the clouds boiling up from it, even in the dark. First it was a pale brown fungus, creeping across the sky to fog the stars. As they crossed the river and climbed the slopes of Dartmoor, the underbelly of the cloud was lit from beneath by sulphurous yellow. They crested a tor warily and skirted the rocks until they could peer below them.

It was a scene from hell. Within a ring of distant orange lights, more furious flashes flew skywards to paint those clouds with lurid colour. The gouts of fire pulsed with a relentless rhythm that imposed itself on their hearts. And between those angry explosions, the clouds of smoke and steam poured unremittingly upwards, smothering the bursts of flame to sullen red and then to bilious yellow.

'It must be Dock,' groaned Honesty, consulting the palm of her hand, as if seeing a map traced there. 'We're not to go anywhere near it. Grandad warned me.'

'I wouldn't want to!' Berlewen shuddered. She could not take her eyes from the pulsing breath of fumes. 'What are they *doing* there?'

'He wouldn't say, even if he knows. But I think… this

is where my father went, looking for my brother. THEY took him away when he was fourteen.'

'You mean, like me? ... If Petal hadn't stopped them.' She reached out in the dark to fondle his shattered ear.

'To serve the Fatherland, they said. Only my father didn't hold with that. He thought he'd found out where they'd taken Colan. There're others besides us who sing the song. He went to try and get him out.'

'What happened?'

'We've never seen either of them since.'

Honesty turned her head resolutely away from the stormy glare. She would not look. She must not let herself be tempted to follow her family.

Berlewen could not drag her own eyes away. The flashes dazzled her. 'We can't win, can we?' she muttered. 'It's hopeless. THEY've got so much power, and we've got nothing. We wouldn't know how to get in or even where to try. We can't just stroll up to the gate, whistling your song. THEY'll have guards everywhere.'

'They say nobody gets in without the summons, except for the guards. And nobody like us comes out alive, unless it's to bury the dead ones.'

The enkenethal growled.

'What do they make inside? It looks like a giant smith's forge, with enormous hammers smashing down on metal, and a huge furnace, and sparks flying. Do you suppose there are really giants with sweat pouring down their faces, bashing out white-hot iron?'

'I'm sure it's much worse than that,' said Honesty in a small voice. 'Humans. THEIR slaves. It gives THEM the things they want. The things we're not allowed to have. The things that give THEM power over us.'

'Like guns?'

The enkenethal growled louder.

'Look out!'

The brilliant flashes and the smouldering clouds had taken their attention from the dark moorland where they stood. They had not seen the swathe of light swinging round the tor behind them, very much closer. Suddenly, through the thump of the factory below, they were aware of the clattering of a large vehicle on the potholed track. Honesty screamed and grabbed at Berlewen's skirt, dragging her into the cleft between the rocks. Petal yelped as his mistress's grip tightened on his ear. He pressed his ungainly body after them. The ridge on his back stood up, quivering with alarm.

Two white lights lit up long shafts of uneven stones and shifting fans of grass and heather. More ominously, another light, set higher, revolved full circle. It swept slowly over the rocks where they crouched, touched the grey mass of the enkenethal's fur and passed on, came round again as the vehicle lurched forward. Probing, searching.

This was not the leaping roar of the vehicle which had brought the summons to Berlewen. It was bigger, grinding its way over the rough moor. As it passed the tor, the girls glimpsed over Petal's shoulders its outline against the stormy sky. It seemed to have no wheels. Its base rolled through the heather like a heavy boat in a choppy sea. As the searchlight swung to the rear, they made out a massive arm, reaching forward from its turret, the long glint of metal.

'Is that a gun, too?' hissed Berlewen. 'That big?'

'It's the lights I'm scared of,' whispered Honesty.

'Do you suppose they're looking for us?'

'It won't matter whether they are or not, if they see us.'

All the time, they watched the tank circling the tor, sweeping its searchlight round and over them. Their knuckles were clenched, their breath louder than they wanted it to be. They were willing the vehicle not to veer off the track and climb the last slope towards them.

'I shouldn't have brought you,' muttered Berlewen. 'It's only me THEY wanted. And Petal.'

'You didn't bring me. I came of my free will, if you remember.'

Since Honesty had put on her brother's breeches and given Berlewen her green and white dress, she was starting to forget to speak to the countess as a chambermaid should. Not that chambermaids were even supposed to be seen by a countess.

She stopped short. The tank had halted. The probing light swivelled in a slow arc, stopped, swung back again.

'I hope that is a gun, and not a sort of nose that can smell,' Berlewen breathed in Honesty's ear. 'They'd pick up Petal at half a mile.'

'Sorry!' he whined softly, pressing against their knees.

The engine roared into violent life. The tank ground forward. For long moments the girls watched the lights swaying, on and on, lower and lower.

'They're going,' Honesty sighed at last. She wiped the sweat from her forehead. 'I thought…'

'So did I.'

Both girls clutched the staffs Map had given them for courage.

'We've got to be miles away from here before dawn.'

All the same, as they struggled eastward over shifting stones and snagging heather, Honesty turned often to stare over her shoulder at the glowering violence of the sky, evidence of the hellhole they were leaving behind them.

Chapter Seven

The heat and the noise were appalling. Over Colan's head the walls of the armaments workshop soared into the dull yellow fog among the roof girders, like dragon's breath. At the level of his workbench the air glowed red from one of many hungry furnaces throughout the shed. Slaves shovelled coal, their backs running with sweat. They threw pails of water in, so that thick sulphurous smoke shot from the edges. The fuel at the centre of the fire turned to a volcano. Other weary boys pounded the foot bellows, on and on, hour after hour. All around Colan, men's arms raised the heavy sledge hammers, pounding white-hot metal as the sparks flew. Another glowing rod came shooting towards him on the conveyor belt, almost too searing for his inadequate gloves to handle. Several times a day, a scream would tell where, at this relentless pace, a gun-barrel had scorched the hands of its unwilling smith. Terror gripped Colan when he heard that. They were all 'hands' in this weapons shop, not humans. If their hands were injured, they were taken away and never seen again, except by the small fatigue party, closely guarded, which was whipped outside to dig a grave for the corpse. That night, there would be a little more space on the crowded concrete floor of the barrack room. Next day, another hand would arrive to fill it.

There was an explosive hiss as he plunged the hot metal into water. Now he must turn it down on the lathe, tapering it fast but exactly, and bore the barrel. Black sulphur oil squirted along its length, as the rod spun rapidly on the lathe. In a moment it would pass out of his hands, to the half-blind boy Gonesek next to him, who must rifle the spiral groove that would make the deadly bullet spin. It was now or never.

Colan's glance flicked up, under thick black lashes. The overseer had his fleshy back turned. The merest nudge of Colan's drill sent the rifle barrel ever so slightly off true. The flash of triumph caught his father's eye at the end of the shed. Luke Olds' job was to lift the finished tubes, inspect them with an accurate eye, pass them on to the next assembly line for the firing mechanism.

A frown of warning drew his father's black brows together. Through the glowing steam and the perspiration dripping from his eyelids, Colan saw his father pick up another barrel, squint expertly along it and pass it on. Was that also one his son had sabotaged?

A glow surrounded Colan's heart, more comforting than the scorching heat of the furnaces. Not every gun would shoot true for the Supreme Council for Justice and Peace.

The warmth of his heart chilled. What had happened to this country, that 'Supreme' excused killing children, 'Justice' was slavery and 'Peace' meant a weapons factory? How had they let it happen?

Under the clanging of furnace doors, the crash of hammers, the hiss of red-hot metal and water, Colan whistled inaudibly the tune whose words he dared not sing aloud.

'And make his land free.'

The barbed ball on the whip lacerated his shirt and scored his shoulders. The blow sent him sprawling over the workbench, so that his horrified face almost struck a length of blazing metal coming towards him. His sweat felt icy for a moment. He had once seen an overseer force a slave's head into a vat of caustic soda. He would never forget those choking screams.

'We must keep our minds on our job, mustn't we, sonny?' grinned the overseer, fondling the bloodied lash.

As Colan's shaking hands resumed their work, he drilled the next barrel accurately and passed it on to his neighbour. The smaller boy looked up at him. One eye was filmed with white, blind. The other gleamed through the steam, startlingly green. Colan knew from the wide black pupil that Gonesek barely saw, even with that one eye. His clever fingers gouged out the rifle groove, measured the spiral, polished it. Yet Gonesek was disturbingly aware of the people around him.

The green eye winked. Colan felt comforted.

Night had long since fallen when Colan and his father trudged their exhausted way back to the barracks with the rest of their shift. Colan's father hummed under his breath, just softly enough for the bad-tempered guard not to hear. The rhythm of the song seemed all that kept Colan's feet lifting one after another and his body more or less upright. He marvelled that his father had the spirit for a tune. His eyes went up to Luke Olds' face, under the merciless yellow lamps. Luke's head was up, though almost everyone else's was drooping between their shoulders. His eyes seemed to see something beyond the lights. But when he turned to force a smile for Colan, his face was haggard, his eyes glinting out of dark hollows. Colan saw the effort that whisper of song had cost him. It seemed all that kept the two of them going.

It was not safe to talk until they were inside the barracks, and perhaps not then. Anyone might buy another week's life as an informer.

The stench met them as soon as the door was opened. There was this one room for two hundred slave workers. There were no bathrooms or toilets. A row of rusting stained buckets stood along one wall. The prisoners emptied them each morning before work, but there was no water to rinse them. There were no mattresses either, or blankets. After the heat of the furnaces, the room struck chill, even in summer. They must lie shivering on the hard floor in the clothes they had worked in.

All the same, Luke Olds stripped off every piece of filthy rag, to which his countryman's garb of smock and breeches had been reduced. He shook them out and raked the dirt from his skin with his fingernails as best he could. The smell of sweat and oil was deep in his pores. He put on his clothes again and combed his hair with his fingers. He grinned at Colan, squatting on the floor with his head over his knees, and kicked him quietly.

'You too, boy. They want to break us. Make us less than human. We won't let them. When I was your age, I'd dodge a proper wash if it wasn't for your Granny scolding me. Not here. We'll keep our self-respect, in spite of them.'

Colan forced himself to his feet and went through the same nightly ritual. Some of the new arrivals still had the strength left to laugh at him. Luke murmured over the bloody cuts on Colan's back. But he picked up his son's hands and examined them more keenly. Four guttering candles were all the light for the crowded, shadowy shed.

'You'll do,' he said, giving them a warm clasp before dropping them. 'Be careful though. Your fingers are your life here. Damage them, and you're... out.'

Colan knew. Those new arrivals had taken the place of slaves too ill or injured to be of further use. If you could not work, even for a day, there was no hospital, no sick leave, no second chance.

He was pulling on the rags of his shirt when slighter hands closed over his, stopping them. Gonesek moved the cloth aside again. His hands were cooler than Luke's, surprisingly soft. He laid his palms over the wounds on Colan's shoulders. His fingertips kneaded the tense muscles above. Colan felt himself beginning to relax, a sense of wholeness creeping back. It always seemed strange that Gonesek, who looked the weakest of them, should have this power.

He turned to smile, and realized that Gonesek could see nothing in this twilight.

'Thanks,' he said, putting the smile into his voice instead.

The cool hands dropped away. Gonesek slumped on to the floor beside him, a small, exhausted figure. Colan wondered guiltily if there was anything he could give him back.

'Doesn't have to be this way!' Luke Olds burst out. 'We had better machines once, so Grandad said. You only had to press a lever and they'd stamp you out anything you wanted. Machines were meant to help you, not grind you down. You could put in a day's work, making things people wanted, and go home at the end of your shift with money in your pocket and still fit to enjoy yourself. It was honest work.'

'So how did it get like this?'

For an instant, Luke looked over his shoulder, then lowered his voice. 'THEY don't want the sort of machines that set you free. THEY don't want us to forget the difference between us and THEM. It's not the guns this factory turns out that are really important. It's scaring us, breaking us, making us think we're nothing, so we forget who we really are.'

There was a silence, broken by the snores of those who had collapsed into weary sleep, and the sobs of some who could not sleep.

'And who are we?'

A snatch of whistled song, bolder, defiant, this time. 'The Prince's friends.'

Chapter Eight

The last shells crashed into the ground. The moor fell silent. A long, long while later the girls and Petal crawled out of the ancient stone grave where they had been hiding from the daylight. A granite pillar that had stood above them lay smashed.

Berlewen stared at the fragments in horror. 'Can guns do this to people?' She fingered the wound in Petal's ear. 'They don't just make holes?'

'Not the big ones.'

'Were they shooting at us?'

'We'd have been mincemeat if they were. Grandad says they come up here to practise on the stones, before they use them on people.'

Twilight was creeping over the last glimpses of the sky.

'I want to get off the moor,' murmured Berlewen. 'I don't want another day like this.'

'We have to go on, anyway. But once we leave Dartmoor, there's roads, farms, strangers. That's a lot more dangerous.'

A week later, the moon was rising only an hour before dawn. It was difficult going in the dark. Sometimes they would risk walking on country lanes.

'There's nobody uses them much, by the look of it, even in daylight,' said Berlewen, stumbling over tall weeds growing up through the track.

'There were more people once,' said Honesty, feeling her way along an overgrown hedge. 'More mouths to feed. All these old fields were full of cows and corn.'

'I wonder what happened to them.'

'There were towns. Like Dock. Didn't your parents tell you that? Thousands and thousands of people, all living in their own houses, street after street. Not just in prison camps, working for THEM. There were places for making things, and shops for selling them. Like a great big market day, all the year round. And schools for the children, and hospitals…'

'What's a hospital? My father and mother never said anything about them.'

'They're not as old as my Grandad.'

'When I was little, I thought it had always been like it is now. Only I remember, one day I was practising archery in the long gallery – well, it was raining outside – and there was a painting of my grandfather, the duke before Papa, all dressed up in clothes of silk and lace, and sitting on a horse. I missed the target. The arrow thunked into the edge of the frame and the portrait jumped off the wall. When I picked it up, I saw there was something else at the back of the painting. Not canvas. A funny sort of paper, stiff and shiny. When I pulled it out and turned it over, it was another picture. Not painted *on*, sort of *in* the shiny paper. There was a man and a woman and a boy. And they weren't dressed like us. More like… well… THEM. He had a jacket and straight trousers, a bit like the suit that horrible man with the purple hair wore. And she had a short and skimpy dress, nowhere near the ground. Mother would have been appalled. And they were standing in front of a... *car*, like THEY drive! I was shocked, because I couldn't think how we came to have a picture of THEM. Only... their faces... they looked like my *family*.'

Honesty's voice came muffled from in front. 'They were. I don't know if I should tell you this, but your family weren't always Grand Dukes and Duchesses of Cornwall. Grandad says your great-grandfather was...'

'*What?*'

'A bank manager.'

'What's a bank?'

'I don't know. But everyone had cars then. Even Grandad's family. And they weren't your servants, begging your pardon, my lady. They rode in aeroplanes to foreign countries for holidays.'

'*Your* family flew in *aeroplanes*? You're making it up.'

'Suit yourself.'

A few minutes later, the chambermaid stopped at a gate. The half moon was creeping over the hill in front of them. It would soon be daybreak. Honesty ran her hands over the silvered gateposts, stopped, moved her fingers back, felt among the shadows.

'We're in luck. A cooked breakfast this morning.'

'What do you mean?'

'Feel this.'

Berlewen's stubbier fingers joined Honesty's thin ones. She felt a plait of straw. Honesty guided her hand along its shape. It had a knobbed head, a narrow twist, then a spreading curve like a skirt.

'Remember that, my lady. Remember it well. If I'm not

with you, it could mean life or death. This is a safe house.'

All the same, their hearts were in their mouths as they eased the heavy farm gate open. Silent though they were, a dog barked fiercely from the yard, as if he smelt the approach of the enkenethal. Berlewen put her hand round Petal's neck, stifling his growl.

The farmhouse was in darkness. No light sprang up in the windows, though those inside must surely have woken. Berlewen pictured the farmer creeping down to the door, reaching for a weapon in the dark, waiting.

Honesty walked across the yard, singing in a small clear voice, *'One new morning our Prince will appear.'*

There was a creak as the door swung open.

'And make his land free,' sang a deeper voice.

There were eggs and bacon in the farmhouse kitchen. Berlewen would not have believed she could eat so much. The enkenethal slumped under the table with a groan of satisfaction, taking with him what looked like a rabbit's head. The black farm dog had refused to stay in the same room with him, cowering in a corner until the farmer put him out in the stable.

After the first hugs of welcome, the farmer's wife cooked their breakfast in silence, as if afraid to ask questions, for fear of the answers they might give. But her eyes continually darted up at them, over cheeks reddened by the fire.

Her husband's face was bright with curiosity. Though he kept his voice low, he could not keep the eagerness out of it.

'It's two years since we had any of the Prince's people through here. Do you think he'll come in our lifetime?

The young one they sing about?' The little bow-legged farmer pushed his red cheeks closer to Berlewen's face. His sloe-black eyes seemed to beg her for reassurance.

'He's got to!' she answered defiantly.

'Which way would you maids be going?' He leaned forward over the table and seemed to hold his breath.

It was Honesty who answered. In their many nights of travelling the chambermaid had become the leader. She seemed to carry a map in her head of a countryside she had never seen before. She had no notes to guide her. Berlewen did not even know if Honesty could read. Their lives depended on her accurate memory of the signs and warnings her grandfather had given them, and perhaps more than their lives.

'Glastonbury,' said Honesty.

Even in this friendly house it felt dangerous to hear that name spoken out loud. There was a gasp of quick-caught breath from the farmer's wife by the stove. Berlewen looked sharply from one to the other of the pair. The farmer shook his head.

'That's what they all said. There's never one come back to tell the tale.'

'How will you get across, two maids like you?' his wife asked.

'And Petal!' said Berlewen, her hand possessively on the enkenethal's rising ruff. Then, as the words sank in, 'Get across what?'

The couple looked at each other. Petal whined.

'The mere.'

'The others must have got across somehow,' Honesty said. 'Else how would the stories get back to Cornwall that that's where the rebels have their camp?'

'You know what's in that mere, do you?'

'I've heard. We have to try. If we want to join the Prince's people, we have to take the risk.'

'Risk of *what*?' Berlewen demanded, jumping to her feet. 'Is nobody going to tell me what you're talking about? I've come to fight. I've got my knife. And if anyone tries to attack me, Petal will have their throat out, won't you?'

The enkenethal barked his enthusiasm.

The farmer's wife held out a bacon rind and stroked his wiry rump. 'He's a fearsome beast, dearie, ugly enough to scare the wits out of a human if he turned nasty. But he wouldn't make more than a mouthful for Her. Like swallowing three blackberries and spitting out the pips, you'd all be, if She was to rise.'

'*She*?'

Both farmer and wife looked round the firelit kitchen. Berlewen was suddenly aware of the thin, scared faces of children poking out under blankets from a truckle bed in the shadowiest corner of the room. The farmer went across to the window and lifted the curtain aside, as though somebody might be listening underneath the sill.

Turning back to the light, he said, 'Us have never seen Her, of course, or we wouldn't be here to tell the tale. But I've seen Her prints. Big enough to lose a cow. Even...' He had to swallow before he could pronounce the word. 'THEY're afraid to come close to the mere. THEY know there's nothing guns and bombs can do against Her sort. My father told me THEY tried it once. She just swallowed THEIR fire and THEIR helicopters fell out of the sky, before She gobbled them up.'

There was a little scream from the children in the bed.

'So THEY leave the mere alone,' nodded his wife. 'THEY're sure there's nobody can get across.'

'That's why it has to be Glastonbury,' said Honesty, with a not-very-successful attempt at boldness. 'It's the one place in all of Britain where THEY are afraid to go. So it's the safest place for the Prince's followers. Even if... some of them get lost in the crossing.' Her voice trailed away, but it strengthened again. 'Anyway, the mere stretches all the way to the Bristol Channel. She can't be everywhere at once, can She? We might be lucky. And there's a causeway, isn't there?'

'Aah. Though much good that will do you, if She hears you coming. The first part's underwater, so THEY can't see it, if THEY ever do come back.'

'And it goes from island to island, all the way to Glastonbury Tor?'

'So my father told me, though I've never set foot on it myself.'

'And you could show us where it starts?'

'I could *tell* you. I wouldn't go within half a mile of it myself.'

'And others have gone that way before us?'

'Those that would rather risk death from Her than stay and serve THEM.'

'They must have got through to the Island of Glastonbury, some of them?'

'Who's to say?'

A log tumbled in the grate. There was a burst of sparks, then the glowing wood began to fade to black.

'The Prince has to be there!' Berlewen cut in. 'Where else *could* he be hiding? He's gathering a secret army and we're going to join him.'

Chapter Nine

The sun was ducking down over the Somerset Levels, a red eye peering through the fingers of willow leaves. Berlewen frowned at it suspiciously.

'It's been so long since we've dared come out in the daytime. Sunlight feels dangerous.'

'I don't think we could find this causeway in the dark. It's going to be bad enough crossing it by twilight. I hope we get there in time.'

'At least they said at the farm there wouldn't be helicopter patrols over the mere.'

'Not since *She* swallowed them out of the sky.'

There was a small silence.

'What *is*… She?'

'The A… Ancoth.' The syllables stumbled off Honesty's tongue. 'The Unknowable One. That's what Map said.'

'Map?'

'I don't suppose you remember him. He's the bootboy at the castle.'

But Berlewen did have a sudden vivid memory of a boy with a pointed chin and freckled nose, holding out a pair of shining boots to her through the hollyhocks. Of a song floating over the garden wall. Of hands closing round hers in the darkness and a startling kiss.

She fingered her staff.

'The boy with the different coloured eyes? The one who cleaned my boots after I threw them at you?'

Honesty nodded dumbly, reminded that Berlewen was the countess and she the chambermaid, which she had mostly been tending to forget lately.

'I'm sorry,' said Berlewen gruffly. 'I was upset. What was that word you said?'

'The Ancoth. But Grandfather calls Her "The Dragon-from-Under".'

'The what? There aren't any dragons.'

'There *weren't* any dragons, before THEM. Map says THEY changed things.'

'But even THEY couldn't manufacture a dragon. It's not like a gun. And the farmer said THEY're terrified of this Ancoth-thingy.'

'THEY didn't *make* Her. I think THEY... *woke* Her.'

Berlewen stopped abruptly. They were only a few steps from the water's edge. 'Could we wake Her?'

'The harm's done. She's already awake. And as far as She's concerned, all humans are the same. THEM, us.'

'She can't blame us for what THEY've done!'

'The way Map explained it, it's the earth She loves. And we're dangerous to it. Humans.'

'But can't we wave a flag or something, to show her we're the goodies?'

'Are we?'

'Of course we are!' Thunder flashed in Berlewen's face.

'Everybody thinks their side are the goodies, don't they? In any war.'

'But we are, aren't we? We've got to believe that! How could we risk danger, death, as rebels if we didn't?'

'If you wanted power and glory more.'

'I just want to be *free*!'

'So do I, but I expect in the end I'll still be a chambermaid.'

Berlewen bit her lip. They narrowed their eyes to stare down the shining track of the evening sun. The wide levels of Somerset were brimming with water. Here and there, tussocks of trees stood out of the flood. Bubbles broke, spilling widening circles. There were plops of fish rising, making the girls' strained nerves start. A heron ghosted low over the surface and glided away under the branches of willow trees. Gnats danced in the still air.

'It must be somewhere here.' Honesty swallowed a lump of fear.

'But is Glastonbury *there*? I can't see anything.'

The golden sun-road lay across the water, but it ended in a wall of mist. Beyond sight, the way might go on for ever, out into the sea, the ocean. Or it might end in bafflement, islets inhabited only by frogs, uncrossable meres, or solid, but hostile land, the territory of THEM again.

'They promised us at the farm it would be here. We have to trust them. They're the Prince's people.'

'But nobody they send ever comes back.'

'We're not going back either, are we? Not till THEY are defeated. Not till the Prince is king.' Honesty stepped briskly down the last slope to the flooded plain.

Petal bounded after her. He lapped at the water's edge, then shook his head violently and spat it out.

'Three willows, and then two, and a fallen trunk between them, half underwater; that's what he said.'

'There,' said Berlewen curtly, pointing.

'I didn't think it would be that easy to find.' Honesty looked suddenly disoriented, doubtful.

Berlewen strode towards it. 'Come on. Let's get on with it.'

Sunlight had bleached the fallen willow trunk to silver-white. It was broad-backed, arching gently as it sloped down into the shallow water, but possible to walk along with care. Berlewen took off her boots and hung them round her neck. She hitched up her dress. Honesty removed her shoes.

'It's warm,' said Berlewen, as the water sidled between her toes. She walked on, treading carefully now that she could no longer see what lay in front of her. 'I wish it wasn't so muddy. What if we get tangled up in branches underwater? It's getting deeper… Oh!'

'What's wrong?' Honesty halted abruptly behind her, her voice sharp with fear.

'I'm off the tree-trunk. I thought I'd fallen. It's up to my knees. But there's something here. It feels… it feels like logs, laid across, like a track. One after the other. It is! We've found the causeway.'

'It's only what he told us about the beginning of the road. We're a long way from finding Glastonbury. And the sun's going down.'

Berlewen turned for a moment. The sun was in her eyes, making her face shine as it met Honesty's. But when she turned back, her shadow fell long in front of her, darkening the way ahead. She walked on.

'The water's getting colder.'

They ploughed along, the muddied water pulling against their legs at every step. An islet rose ahead of them, a tangle of alders and rowans, twisted roots confusing the underwater track. Honesty skirted one side of it, Berlewen the other.

'Here,' called the chambermaid. 'It goes this way.'

'Wait!' Berlewen caught her up and clutched her arm as Honesty stepped out into the water on the far side. 'Is that… *it*?'

The sky stood palest blue over the levels of mist. Light was draining from it, touching the cloud with pale gold. Far ahead that sunset cloud seemed to hunch together, become more solid, as though there might be something darker behind its brilliant sheen.

'It *could* be a hill,' Honesty said in a small hopeful voice. 'A tall hill. Would Glastonbury look like that?'

'As long as it's not…'

'The path goes straight towards it.' Honesty waded on.

The sun sank down below the western hills behind them. The level mere was still filled with light, but less certain, losing the definition of sun and shadow, colder. Overhead, the sky held its glory of blue and gold for a little longer. In front, the twilight was closing in their horizon. Whatever had bulked behind the mist was gone now.

'How long have we got before it's really dark?'

'With this mist, less than an hour. But we can't see the track, anyway. Now that we've found it, we can feel it in the dark.'

'I don't think I want to be here in the dark.'

They passed a second islet. It was shallower here. The

water barely splashed around their ankles. They walked side by side.

'Do you think we're getting close? There are no lights ahead.'

'There wouldn't be, would there? For the rebels, it's life or death.'

'Will there be sentries?'

'Of course.'

'We don't know the password.'

Honesty started to whistle. The lilt of the Prince's song, like a promise, wandered away across the darkening water. Petal barked an enthusiastic refrain.

'Hush, you fool!' Berlewen's hand grabbed his ruff.

'Sorry! S-sorry!' His big paws splashed on doggedly. But the moment seemed to have loosed him from his mournful lethargy. When a coot sailed past, red legs paddling her black body towards her nest, the enkenethal launched his uncoordinated length through the shallows after her. She took off in panic and still he pursued her, vainly bounding. Showers of spray somersaulted into the sky. The girls were soaked before he had spattered his way out of range. There was a tremendous splash. He must have found deeper water, for he was swimming away, tail thrashing in his violent wake.

'Petal! Petal! Come back!' screeched Berlewen.

Honesty whistled.

Waves were washing around them from his retreating commotion. Clouds of pigeons and crows took off from the wooded islets, chattering and screaming their disapproval. Silence and secrecy were shattered.

'We've got to get him back,' said Honesty. 'Get him under control, quick.'

'How?'

But Berlewen waded after him as fast as she could. The broken water was subsiding now. She could no longer see the enkenethal. The sunken logs of the causeway lay far behind her.

Suddenly the muddy surface beneath her feet was no longer there. She tumbled forward into water out of her depth, letting go of her staff. She went under, fighting her way up to air and light. The water had an unexpected taste of salt.

In those few moments under the water, the world seemed to have grown suddenly dark. She was treading water now, in no danger of drowning. But she could not see back to the causeway where she had left Honesty. She had long since lost sight of Petal. She was swimming in a closed circle of lonely water.

She opened her mouth to call, and closed it again. What was she afraid of? She listened for Honesty's voice. There was no sound. Why had the racket of birds fallen so utterly silent?

She felt, rather than heard, it coming. The whole bed of the mere seemed to heave under her. A huge rearing wave lifted her up and rolled her skywards, leaving her stomach lurching behind. Slowly she slid down the face of the wave and heard a hollow sucking from below. A shudder followed, the slap of waves on a far shore. Just for a moment she thought she heard Honesty cry out, a thin and distant wail. Then there was a roar in her ears, that was not the water or the rush of wind, before the lake rose again. She was tossed like a cork, helpless.

In her terror, Berlewen expected fire and smoke, but the water grew very cold. Her mind was now a limitless void of blackness. No thought would come but horror, no name to make it manageable. At last the blood beating in her ears drummed out an awful syncopation. '*The Ancoth. The Ancoth...*' The thing that even THEY had fled from.

Rigid with shock, she began to sink, then flailed wildly in self-preservation. Did the words boom through the waters or in her head?

'UNCLEAN! UNCLEAN!'

The current seemed to be sucking her towards a shore now. In almost darkness she was aware of sharp white rocks slanting up. The water frothed between them, slid slimily out to tow her in to them. She could not swim against it. There would be a beach inside those rocks, dry land, refuge, if she could squeeze unwounded past their sharp white edges.

Close enough now to hear the gurgling of this channel. A glimpse of glistening red and black, arched like a cavern. Where were the trees, the shingle, the reed beds? A tunnel too vast to take in at a single look, fringed with a dripping curtain of mottled softness horribly like dark flesh. The paralysing chill of the water, puckered now by an exhalation of fetid wind.

Berlewen knew, and must not know, where she was being sucked. In the last trace of vanishing sunlight its skin gleamed dull green. The eyes – those orbs must be eyes, though they were enormous – glistened as though they caught the sun that no longer shone on Berlewen below. She could see veins in the eyes, like roads of blood, two circles of brilliant gold, then tunnels of fathomless black. Strange, that even as the chill horror of the Ancoth was about to swallow her in, she could see that its eyes were beautiful. Beautiful and terrifying. They were so far above her. Did they see her? Did the Ancoth even know she was swallowing Berlewen St Kew Trethevy? Or care?

In another moment she would be swept in under the overhanging jaw. The slithering tongue would gulp. She would be sucked down beyond air, beyond light, smothered, swallowed, acid beginning to dissolve her body even as she drowned. Would the teeth grind her first?

She was almost at that reef. The light was going.

'*Help!*' she cried. 'Save me!'

Chapter Ten

There was a sudden jolt of the waves, like a gigantic hiccup. Berlewen found herself washed further out. The enormous eyes stared down at her. They seemed to focus, surprised.

'Please, don't swallow me!' she shouted desperately. 'I'm on your side. I'm against THEM. I'm trying to get to the Prince's rebels at Glastonbury.'

She was babbling in terror. It seemed impossible that the Ancoth could understand her. This was some dark terrible thing, woken by violence. Violence to the earth. Wasn't that what Honesty had told her?

Again the words hammered in her ears. She could not tell if the massive throat had actually spoken them.

'YOU ARE *THEM*.'

'I'm not! I'm not! I'm Berlewen St Kew Trethevy, Countess of Tintagel. THEY made my father lord over the peasants, but it doesn't mean we're THEM. We have to do what THEY tell us, like everyone else. We're no different from the Olds, like Honesty. THEY sent me a letter. I was to go to THEM. Do you know what that means? I'd have to serve THEM until the day I died. So I ran away. I'm for the Prince.'

The words raced on. Berlewen hardly knew what she was saying. Anything to prolong this moment, when she was outside the waiting jaws, when there might be the faintest chance that the monster was listening.

Something huge moved beneath her. It must be a gigantic foreleg. The horrid head lifted clear of the water so that Berlewen surged up on a vast wave and slid back again between two monstrous gnarled shoulders. The dripping head gazed down at her with a huge sadness. Or was it indifference?

Again words seemed to come from inside herself. She did not know if it was she or the Ancoth who was the one forming them.

'YOU ARE NOT LIKE THE OLDS. You threw your boot at the girl and soiled her washing. You shouted at the gardener, who was growing vegetables for you.'

'That wasn't my fault.' She wept tears of anger and indignation, as well as shock. 'I was the countess and they were servants. I was brought up to shout at people. I didn't know...'

'*THEY* SHOUT AT PEOPLE, TO GET WHAT THEY WANT. *THEY* FOUL THE EARTH. IT IS BECAUSE YOU ARE LIKE *THEM* THAT YOU WERE CHOSEN TO BECOME ONE OF *THEM*.'

That thought had never entered Berlewen's head before. It shocked her now. Too quickly to ask herself whether there could be any truth in it, she cried out, 'No! How dare you! I'd never be one of THEM!'

A roar shattered the falling night. A blast of icy wind shot from the gullet. Waves smashed into her face. She screamed and went underwater, swallowed a mouthful of mud and slime and came up gasping. Was it the lake which was still shuddering around her or her own scared flesh?'

'I'm a rebel!' she spluttered. 'I'm running *away* from THEM. I'm going to fight THEM.'

'WASTING MY EARTH.'

'For a good cause. For the Prince. To kill his enemies.'

The Ancoth roared again. She heaved closer, stood high over the girl, leaned down Her jaws. A gale was churning the water around Berlewen, blinding her with foam.

'Look at you. *You're* angry. And you swallow your enemies.' Berlewen yelled a last defiance.

The lake grew still. The huge eyes clouded. The tempest sucked back inside the closing jaws. There was deep darkness, chill water. Berlewen was more afraid before the silence and the stillness than in the blast and storm. The fear reached to the very core of her being. She dared not argue now.

The silence was split by a wild barking. Berlewen's lips moved in a silent plea. *No, Petal! No! Don't come and find me. Not now.*

The lidded eyes half opened. Through the water that buoyed her up, Berlewen was aware of a sudden contraction in the Ancoth's limbs, a tenseness, waiting, listening.

'It's nothing,' said Berlewen rapidly. 'Just my enkenethal. I was searching for him. He chased a coot, you see, and I lost sight of him. That's why I left the causeway, to look for him. But it doesn't matter! You don't want him. You want me. Petal's got nothing to do with THEM. It's only me. You're right. I'm nearly... I'm as bad as THEM. Let's get it over with. I don't know what you do to THEM. Drown them. Eat them. Only make it quick. Please!'

The eyes were enormous now, glinting, flickering with light. The jaws were beginning to open, the wind coming stronger on her face.

There was a frantic splashing to her right. An indignant squawking of ducks. But the noise of swimming came on.

'*Stay*, Petal! *Stay!*' All the authority the countess could command rang in her shout.

The enkenethal crashed closer.

'Go back! Go back!' she shrieked at him. 'You bad animal. I don't want you.'

But she was longing to clasp his furry neck in her arms.

'Sorry! Sorry!' he gasped, butting into her and knocking her underwater. He dived and gripped her clothes with his teeth and hauled her up again. 'S-sorry!'

She hugged him silently, tears flowing. 'Oh, Petal. Why did you come? Why do you love me so much? What have I done to you?'

The hanging snout of the Ancoth leaned closer. Cool air fanned their faces.

'Hello!' yelped the enkenethal. 'I didn't see you. Sorry!'

Berlewen clasped Petal closely.

The voice shuddered. 'YOU KNOW THIS... HUMAN?'

'Yes! She saved me from the hunters when I was a pup.' Petal licked Berlewen's face with enthusiasm.

'SHE LOVES YOU, THEN?'

'Yes! Yes!' Petal was ecstatic

'SHE WOULD HAVE DIED FOR YOU.'

'Sorry! Sorry!' he yelped.

'Oh, Petal. I tried. I didn't want both of us to die. I'm not worth it.'

The enkenethal growled in a ludicrous imitation of the Ancoth's roar. That roar now drowned it out. Berlewen and Petal clutched each other tight.

'YOU *LOVE* HER?'

Petal's barking rose to a frenzy.

'THEN SHE IS YOURS, ENKENETHAL! NOT BECAUSE SHE LOVED YOU. BECAUSE YOU LOVE HER.'

The mere settled into stillness, grew dark, silent.

'Is that... all?' Berlewen could hardly believe it. 'I can go on? To Glastonbury?'

The hill of flesh was sinking out of the sky, revealing the stars. The water sighed and swished as the vast body submerged little by little under the black surface. The waves washed higher, lifting Berlewen and Petal up and up, still clasped together, trembling with joy and relief. There was an explosion of foam as the jaws went under, a flash of golden light from the brilliant eyes, though the sun had long since set. Then cold again. Wet clothes and fur, a chill night breeze. And Honesty calling.

Chapter Eleven

There was a boat. Berlewen did not remember hearing it coming, but hands were hauling her on board. The frail craft of withies and skin almost overturned as the massive paws of the enkenethal flailed for a footing and his sodden shoulders heaved the length of his uncoordinated body on board. Honesty was sitting in the stern. She ducked as Petal shook himself over her and then bailed the water out rapidly.

There were two others in the boat. An older man, his slouch hat shadowing his face, held Berlewen steady and helped her to a seat in the bows. From behind him she caught a strong whiff of cow dung. She wrinkled her nose and turned her head. She glimpsed a boy, his hand wary on the single oar with which he steadied the craft.

'You woke Her,' the man said solemnly. 'We knew from the waves that washed up to Glastonbury.'

'And yet you put out in this little boat,' said Honesty. 'That was brave.'

'You've Gawen here to thank for that. Just about to start supper, we were. He was bringing in the milk from the cowshed, when he heard the breakers crashing on the shore. He put down the buckets he was carrying and was back out into the night before we could stop him.'

There was a soft laugh from the stern. 'You weren't far behind me, Tom.'

The starlight touched him. Berlewen started. Just for a moment, she seemed to be staring again into the black cavern of the Ancoth's eye. Then she saw that it was an eye-patch, darkening one side of the boy's face. The other eye glinted brightly at her in the silver light. 'Better than a guard dog, Her-From-Under is. We always know when someone's coming. Or trying to.'

'But suppose it hadn't been us,' Honesty insisted. 'What if it had been THEM coming?'

'Then there'd have been nobody left for us to worry about.'

'And… if it's a friend? Does She always let them through?'

'Depends. She might; She might not. It's not whether they're friends to us; it's whether She feels they're friends to *Her*. She let *you* pass, by the look of you.' He smiled at Honesty. 'You've barely got the bottom of those breeches wet.'

'It was me,' said Berlewen, in a small voice. 'It was me She was going to swallow. I never thought… She took me for one of THEM.'

'I'd have told Her different,' Honesty said indignantly.

'No. That's what's so awful. I think… I think She might be right.'

'You're saying you're a traitor? You'd betray us?' The older man's voice was sharp with warning.

'Steady, Tom,' young Gawen laughed. 'She's here, isn't she? Alive. Her-From-Under wouldn't have let her go if she was a danger to the land.'

There was something reassuring in the way he turned his head to smile at her. Oddly enough, it made her argue with herself.

'But I was. I might have been. Oh, maybe I still am!'

'Never!' said Honesty. 'I nearly had to stop you fighting THEM over this daft enkenethal.'

Berlewen hugged the soaking Petal close. They were both shivering. 'He's all that saved me. I never worried that I was ordering people about like THEM. And the worst thing She said – at least, I *think* She must have said it; it was in my head – was that... if I'd got to Headquarters... Well, I thought I'd be THEIR slave, a prisoner, treated horribly... only... I never thought THEY might want to make me one of THEM.'

'THEY couldn't, unless you wanted it,' said the boy quickly, sculling across the night water by the faintest gleam of stars.

Berlewen looked up at him, her gaze straight and true. 'I might have wanted to. I might have liked seeing everyone afraid of me, making them do what I said. Power.'

'You're wiser than you think,' he said, his one eye regarding her with equal seriousness. 'You can see how stupid you sometimes are. That's the beginning of wisdom.' And then his bright eye smiled deep into hers.

'Watch out, Gawen!' called Tom from the bows. 'We're coming into the Brue.'

The slight slither of water past the sides gathered speed. A current was rippling and plopping along the sides. Gawen standing in the stern, bent to his long oar more strongly and concentrated on steering them across the flowing stream. They had left the little reedy islets behind. The stars gleamed brighter on the open water. Ahead the sky was misted over with silver radiance. A huge dark dragon shape loomed up before them. A hill dizzyingly high after the water levels. They made out the long ridged back of a far larger island.

'Is this Glastonbury? Is that where the true Prince is?' breathed Berlewen. 'Will I really meet him?'

The man and the boy exchanged glances over her head.

'There's Selevan,' said Tom. 'He's our leader.'

'And he's going to lead the rebels against THEM? We're going to fight THEM!' Her voice rose.

'So he says.'

'If She lets us.'

'Wouldn't She?' demanded Berlewen.

'Who's to say?'

Gawen had heaved them out of the current now. They were slipping more easily under the nearer slopes of the shadow. Honesty was leaning forward eagerly, trying to peer through the darkness.

Berlewen had turned back to the enkenethal. She gripped him so hard that he yelped.

'Sorry!' he gasped automatically, and licked her face.

'Petal saved my life,' Berlewen said, with a long shudder. '*He's* why She let me go. It was almost as though they were two of a kind, Petal and the Ancoth. They understood each other. I've never heard him say anything except "Sorry" before to me. I sort of thought... I hoped She might be letting me go because I loved Petal. Because I didn't want him to be all brave and stupid and die for me. I told Her to take me instead. And She should have done. But that wasn't why She changed her mind. It wasn't because I deserved it for loving Petal. I've just realized what She said. She let me go because *Petal* loved *me*.'

'It's as good a reason as any,' Gawen's voice came out of the darkness, over his shoulder.

Petal sat up very straight, his hideous snout proudly erect against the stars. Berlewen laid her wet head on his equally wet shoulders. The enkenethal panted ecstatically.

There was a murmur of voices ahead, though no lights showed. Hands seized the boat and drew it up the beach. There were male and female voices, low, efficient, going through a routine carried out many times.

As she stumbled to her feet, Berlewen reached out her hand and started with shock. Her staff was missing, Map's gift, lost in the marsh. She shot a glance in the starlight at Honesty. The chambermaid was still grasping hers.

Minutes later they were safely ashore and inside a house the like of which Honesty and Berlewen had never seen before.

It was hollowed out from the earth itself. Its sod roof sat almost on the ground, leaving just enough height for them to duck under and in at a low door. The girls could see that even in broad daylight it must appear no more than a swelling of turf and bracken. There were no windows. As they stepped down into it, a few scattered candles gave small peeps of illumination, the jut of someone's chin, a fall of hair, a wooden platter on a scrubbed table. No hint of light would escape outside.

Even the fire no more than smouldered, wisps of smoke caught under the rafters. In the daytime, Honesty guessed, even that would be smothered under turfs.

As they grew accustomed to the shadows, they became aware that there were about thirty people in the room, men, women, a few older children still awake and wary as the adults. In a few terse sentences, Tom told their story. Berlewen waited for Gawen to join in and describe her encounter with the Ancoth. But when she looked round, he had slipped away into the background. As she watched, he came staggering back with an armful of logs. He knelt down in the ashes of the hearth and began rousing the fire. She felt a lurch of disappointment. Seeing Gawen in the boat, with the rakish patch over one eye, she had hoped he might have been one of the fighters, a young rebel hero. Instead, he was only a servant, smelling of the cowshed.

He stood up, wiping his hands on his stained breeches, and began talking to one of the women. Soon she appeared at Berlewen's side bearing a woollen towel and dry clothes. She led the girl to the side of the long low room, where woven hurdles separated a sleeping compartment. Berlewen changed into the rough shirt and tunic. The fire was burning brighter now and the woman set the wet clothes to dry. The enkenethal already lay flopped out in exhaustion on the hearth, the inside of his purple ears glowing pink, his coat steaming.

There was an argument going on. Tom, who seemed to be in charge here, was on his feet, but other voices were questioning him. Their faces were shadowed from her.

'So, do we keep them or throw them back?'

Berlewen started. While she had been away, the discussion seemed to have taken a turn she had not expected. She flashed with indignation. Had she and Honesty walked all this way, braved so much danger, defied the orders of THEM and got past the Ancoth, only to be rejected by a pack of peasants?

The enkenethal lifted his head and whined. Then he flopped into sleep once more. Berlewen bit back her rage and kept silent. It was Honesty who spoke.

'You don't have to keep us. I can see we may not be much use. But Grandad said Glastonbury was the only place left, if we didn't want THEM to get her ladyship… Berlewen.' She shot an apologetic glance at her former mistress. 'And Prince.' She said the last name fondly, looking over her shoulder at the enkenethal, who panted in his sleep and wagged the tip of his tail.

'Prince?' said a man, spluttering with laughter. 'Is that what you call him?'

'I hope that's not your idea of joke,' muttered a woman.

'No,' said Honesty, blushing as they all looked at her. 'It's not a joke. It's just… well, the hunt killed his mother. He was the only one left. And when they brought him to live at the castle… it made all the difference.' Her voice trailed into a whisper. 'He… loved me. Like our Prince would… But Berlewen calls him Petal.'

There was louder laughter. Berlewen was glad of the feeble candlelight. She was blushing too.

'Is he well-trained? Can he keep quiet?' someone asked.

There was silence from the girls.

'He's a friend of Her-From-Under,' came Gawen's voice from low in the shadows. Berlewen turned. The boy was at the table behind her, cutting bread. He winked at her with his one brown eye.

'Aye,' said Tom. 'He's why She let them through.'

Thirty heads were turned towards the sprawl of rough fur and slack sinews, darkening the rushes before the fire. Petal slept in innocence under their stares. He snored loudly.

There was a longer silence, in which something seemed to be understood. Then Tom moved decisively. 'We're poor hosts. These travellers haven't had a bite of supper yet. It'll be tomorrow before we know where we are.'

'Soup's coming to the boil now.'

A saucepan lid clanked as Gawen lifted it from the fire. A wonderful smell of leeks filled the air. Hunks of bread appeared at the girls' elbows, wooden goblets of milk. Then there were blankets behind the hurdle screen, a straw mattress, sleep. They left Petal warm by the smothered fire.

Chapter Twelve

It should not have surprised Colan when his father fell ill. Sooner or later most slaves did. The work was so heavy, the factory floor so hot with steam and sweat, the barracks so cold, the food so thin, the water dirty. The guards beat their captives sadistically for sheer spite. The spirits of some prisoners broke first and their resistance collapsed. Others struggled to preserve their self-respect until their bodies broke under the strain. Luke Olds was of the latter sort. There was a kind of disbelief in Colan, as he watched the hard flesh of his father's outdoor life drain away and leave a gaunt skeleton beginning to stoop over his inspection bench like an old man. He had a rattling cough, which disturbed Colan even in his sleep of exhaustion, as they lay side by side on the damp hard floor.

'How long?' Colan groaned to himself. 'How long do we have to suffer like this?'

But when he looked at the teams of guards changing shifts, rested and well-fed, their round pink cheeks fresh as children's, at the blank perimeter walls climbing into the sky, topped by jagged glass, at the locked gates guarded by men with guns, there seemed no reason why it should ever end.

How many of THEM must there be, to keep a whole country down like this? he wondered.

In his helpless anger, he wanted to distort every gun barrel he made for THEM. But it was more dangerous now than it had been. He dared not send a faulty piece for his father to inspect. As soon as a slave began to weaken, the guards watched him.

It could only be a matter of days now. Colan looked up from his own work, risking the lash across his shoulders for even turning his eyes like this. He saw his father stagger and recover himself. He must have been standing at his work for four hours. The day stretched on ahead. Colan hit the barrel before him a savage hammer blow.

The clang of metal rang out above the constant din. At once, the overseer was at his back, saw the flattened steel and screamed abuse as he dragged Colan into the centre of the floor. There was a platform there, from which the overseers could watch the benches round them. Colan was thrown forward, so that his upper body bent over the wooden boards. The ragged shirt was torn from his back. In spite of himself, he screamed as the lash came down, again and again, each blow more agony as the skin was stripped from raw flesh.

'That's naughty, that is, a spoilt barrel. You make guns for THEM and you make them perfect. Get it?'

The kick almost broke his knee.

'Yes, sir. I'm very sorry, sir. My hand slipped. It won't happen again, sir.'

He hated himself. It was no use saying anything else. Even abject humility might not be enough to save his life. He clenched his body against what would happen next.

There was a clatter, a loud splash and a scream, from where other slaves were degreasing the barrels with a boiling solution of caustic soda. With an oath, the overseer leaped off his dais, his whip already flailing.

Colan stood for a moment, dazed by his reprieve. Then he limped back to his bench. He hunched over his work, trying to make himself invisible. Many of the guards would have executed him on the spot for that mistake. He must concentrate. What sense or hope was there in mutiny? It needed every ounce of strength and wit for a slave to stay alive.

Through the sweat pouring between his eyes, he risked another glance at his father. This time, though, he was careful to move only his eyes, not turn his head. Luke was paler than ever today, in spite of the heat. He was looking at his son, between the inspection of the finished barrels. He shouldn't do that. Keep your eyes on your own work, Colan prayed. The flogging he had just endured endangered his father's life as well as his own.

He must be more careful in future. Too risky to send any more warped barrels on their way, knowing his father would let the defect pass and another flawed weapon would make its small defiant stand against the might of the oppressor. There was an overseer hovering near Luke. Too near, too watchful. Colan could see that he was waiting for the slightest excuse to pull the older man out of the line. If that happened, his father would not return.

Luke Olds, with the clear, brave eyes. Luke Olds, a middle-aged man in a slave-labour barracks, where most young men did not survive beyond their twenties. Luke, who would whistle, almost under his breath, the Prince's song when a fellow-slave was on the point of collapsing.

It was his father now who looked ready to collapse at any moment.

As the next hot length of steel hissed towards him, Colan bent his eyes to his task. But as he tore them from his father's anguished face, his glance passed over the slighter boy working at his side. In that moment, Gonesek turned his own face momentarily to Colan. One blind white eye, filmed with sweat. The other green, blazing with a shared anger.

Chapter Thirteen

It seemed strange to be venturing out in the light of day, after two weeks of travelling only at night. Mist rose from the meres that surrounded Glastonbury, so that the asymmetrical tor stood out into the summer sky like a separate island. Sun glinted on a ruined abbey.

'I don't understand,' Berlewen frowned as they walked away from the hidden hut. 'Last night, when he rescued us, I thought Gawen must be one of their heroes. He was so brave. But this morning, the men are all out at weapon practice and, look, there's Gawen herding the cows. He's just a farmhand, after all.'

They turned to watch. Through the willow trees the boy was encouraging the beasts out to pasture with a loving slap on the rump. Their breath steamed in the morning air.

'I know what you mean, about expecting more. He reminds me of Map,' said Honesty. She caught Berlewen's puzzled face. 'Yes, well, I know Map's only your bootboy and general dogsbody, but he's a *good* bootboy. He makes the boots really shine. And he's been good to me too.'

'I'm looking for a hero, not a bootboy or a cowherd.

In a camp of rebels, "cowherd's" another name for coward.'

'I still think I'd ask Gawen if I needed help. I feel... *safe* with him.'

Petal wagged the whole of his rear end.

'But it's fighters like Tom who will lead the rebellion. And... Selevan. Isn't that what they called him, their chief?' Berlewen's eyes began to shine. 'Do you suppose Selevan really is the Prince?'

'We won't know until we see him this morning, at this big meeting.'

'Will we know, then?'

Honesty looked startled. 'If he is the Prince, we'd be bound to, wouldn't we? I mean, we've all been singing the Prince's song so many years, longing for him to come. We'd have to be sure when we were in his presence, that this was the real thing at last.'

'How?'

'I don't know,' Honesty mumbled. 'Just... a feeling.'

The pale stone of a ruined abbey lifted pointed arches above the green turf. Apple trees nodded beyond, shedding their early windfalls. Further off, Glastonbury Tor climbed in grassy terraces to the single pinnacle of a tower as the mist was clearing. They walked towards it.

Petal barked. At the same moment Honesty heard the low whine in the sky.

'It's THEM! That's a helicopter coming! THEY know we're here!'

'Don't be daft. That farmer said THEY don't fly over the mere. THEY're too scared of the Ancoth. THEY won't come near us.'

Still they ran. They raced through the long grass of the

apple orchard and threw themselves under the low-hanging branches. Petal sat between them, shivering, as though in the grip of nightmare. Berlewen fondled the bullet wound in his ear and squeezed him in a silent hug.

The sound droned away into the far trails of mist. There was only birdsong, and the sudden rise of voices, where others were gathering towards the same point as themselves.

'Lucky for us THEY can't imagine that anyone could ever get past the Ancoth.' Berlewen's voice held a note of pride, almost as though it had been her own achievement.

'If Glastonbury's really safe from THEM, I wonder why the rebels need to fight. Why don't they just build a new kingdom, right here?'

'And let THEM get away with it? Rule the rest of the country?'

Honesty's face went slowly white. She put her hand to her mouth and whispered, 'How could I even think that? With everyone else out there? Those factories. Father, Colan.'

Both girls were silent, remembering the yellow glare over Dock, the roiling smoke, the thump and clang of metal on metal beating out weapons, the shells exploding, the people who never came back.

They joined the crowd making for a low entrance at the foot of the tor. Sentries looked them over strangely, but Tom had given them a password and they were ushered through.

They went down into a much bigger underground hall. Sawn-off tree-trunks held up the rafters. Honesty could see the white roots of grass snaking down out of the sod roof, vainly seeking more soil. Candles were needed even in daytime, but they could burn more and unshaded when any escaping light would be swallowed up in the brightness outside. The floor was packed. Benches were arranged in semicircles, for the older people. The rest, men, women and children, sat hunkered on the rush-strewn earth in front of them. As the girls stood wondering where to go, one familiar face turned to them from the crowd of strangers. Gawen was squatting with the rest of his hut. He winked at them with his one bright brown eye. The girls squeezed in beside him.

There was a rustle of expectation. Faces turned up in the candlelight, towards the dais. A dozen rebels, men and women, filed up the steps and sat at the trestle table. The girls recognized only the grey-haired Tom, who had rescued them with Gawen last night.

'Which is Selevan?' murmured Berlewen.

Honesty scanned the line of faces. She shook her head doubtfully.

Tom knocked on the table with a hammer. 'Silence for our chief.'

There was a rush of whispering, like surf on shingle, and then stillness.

The tall man next to Tom rose. Black hair swept back from his high forehead. His face was gaunt, grave. His dark eyes burned. He looked as if youthfulness might have been robbed from him early. He leaned towards them, his head stooped forward, as though his height was too great for this low-roofed hall.

'*Him?*' whispered Berlewen. 'Is that the Prince?' She

was leaning forward too, her eyes brilliant.

Honesty was silent, like everyone else, intent on listening for his first words.

'Friends!' A rare smile flashed out, giving all of them equality with him. It made their hearts feel warm, their spirits lift. 'In the name of God, welcome! You have won a great victory, simply by being here today. Many times we feared our camp had been betrayed. But THEY no longer believe anyone could get safe across the mere. THEY are afraid to fly over Glastonbury Tor. Do you realize what that means, friends? We have proved that THEY are not all-powerful!'

A cheer roared up from the mass of rebels. In the enclosed space, the earth itself seemed to shake. Petal burst into uncontrollable barking.

'Hush! Hush!' begged Berlewen, embarrassed.

Gawen reached out a hand and laid it on the enkenethal's bristling neck. Petal gave a loud hiccup and relapsed into silence, licking the farm boy's hand.

'Sorry!' he whispered. He flopped down, his heavy head hitting Honesty's lap.

Selevan held up his hand. The hall hushed. The tall leader came round to the other side of the table, as though he wanted nothing to stand between him and his people. He held out his hands to them, his face eager as a boy's. 'We do not have weapons like THEIRS, only bows, spears, knives. You are our real strength, your hearts, your spirits. More and more of you keep coming, escaping from THEIR tyranny. Only last night, we had two recruits from Cornwall.' His smile searched out Tom's people and found Berlewen's eyes. Pride flamed through her whole being. Selevan drew himself up straight then, tall, commanding. 'The time has come for us to rise up and take THEM on!'

There was a burst of wild cheering. People scrambled to their feet, raising their fists. Berlewen was among them, shouting her heart out.

But others looked scared. 'THEY've got guns, tanks. THEY'd crucify us!'

'We're safe enough here.'

Selevan stooped towards them, the smile gone. 'I have been preparing you for something more than safety. Will you join me and free our country?'

His eyes held them. The storm of cheering swept the hall again. It was hard for anyone to stand against it.

Tom, who seemed to be his second-in-command, stepped forward. 'I can tell by your cheers you agree with us. Right. The first thing we need to do is liberate some real weapons – to say nothing of the poor wretches who make them. So we propose to make our first attack on the Dock armaments factory.'

Honesty started so violently that Petal yelped. The Dock factory, where her father and her brother Colan were enslaved – if they were still alive.

'Get away! We'd never get in there,' said a square-shouldered woman from Tom's hut. 'I should know. THEY've got my son. Have you ever seen it? THEY've got walls a mile high and iron gates and guards with guns all over the place.'

Selevan turned towards her, his gaunt face burning now with inner passion. 'So we must get word inside of what we're planning. The slaves must rise at the same time we attack outside. The guards will be caught between us. Yes, we shall lose people. But every gun we seize from THEM tips the odds in our favour. And there are thousands inside that factory.'

Hope was passing from eye to eye, and fear too.

At the far end of the Council table a woman stood up, a coil of silver hair around her head. Her voice trembled a little as she faced Selevan, but her chin was up. 'I say this is folly. I said so when you proposed this to the Council, and I say so now. THEY have these things they talk into. THEY can speak to each other across the sky, hundreds of miles away. Even suppose we could all get to Dock without anyone noticing us, the moment we attacked, THEIR Headquarters would know. Before we could turn round, THEY'd drop death on us out of the sky – bombs, fire, the lot. THEY'll squash us like flies.'

Selevan smiled at her. 'Yes, Livvy. We need wits to counter brute strength. We must make THEM believe Dock is only a diversion, that we are going to attack in strength somewhere else – perhaps Headquarters itself. THEY won't bother too much about protecting the factory from a bit of play-acting. We *can* do it, with God on our side, if we keep faith.'

Tom agreed. 'THEY're not as strong as they'd like us to believe. THEY don't even trust each other. That's what evil does to you. There's only a core of crack fighters around THEM they can really rely on. If you don't believe me, ask Gawen. He was a slave at Headquarters, servicing THEIR vehicles, until he escaped. That's where he lost his eye.'

Honesty's own pale blue eyes grew round with awe as she turned to the boy beside her. 'You never told us!'

He raised his visible eyebrow with a teasing grin. 'You never asked.' Yet in the candlelight the black eyepatch loomed like a cavernous wound.

'And how are we supposed to make THEM believe different from what we intend?' the same square-shouldered woman objected from behind the girls. 'Is somebody just going to walk up to Headquarters and say so? THEY'd never believe us. Whoever it was would end up in a torture cell.'

There was an uneasy silence.

Berlewen broke it. She stood up. With fingers that trembled with passion, rather than fear, she drew a smudged and stained scroll from the inside of her borrowed shirt and held it over her head. 'I've got a summons from THEM. It's been in the water, but you can just about read it still. It says I have to report to Headquarters. I didn't. My enkenethal attacked THEIR messengers, so we ran away together. But I've got the letter. I can still go. I could make up a story about why I'm late. Say you kidnapped me, but I escaped. Then I could tell THEM your plans – the false ones, of course.'

'Would THEY fall for that?' Livvy, the silver-haired Councilwoman sounded unconvinced.

There was a pause, muttered argument. Berlewen was very conscious of Selevan staring down at her, as though she was suddenly the most important person in the hall.

'THEY might believe you. I'm afraid some do go over to the enemy.'

'Usually the toffs,' someone called.

There was a rumble of anger.

'I *am* a… toff.' Berlewen called back. 'I am Berlewen St Kew Trethevy, Countess of Tintagel.' She managed to look both proud and embarrassed. She was not prepared for the reaction.

'A flaming countess!'

'Next thing to one of THEM.'

'Collaborator!'

Petal leaped to his feet beside her, shoulder-high, baring his fearsome teeth.

Selevan held up his hand. Before his silent authority, even Petal quietened. 'Have you forgotten so soon?' His gaze sought Berlewen out and held her. 'She strayed from the causeway to find her enkenethal. The Dragon-From-Under almost swallowed her. But the enkenethal spoke up for her and the Dragon-From-Under let her pass. Would you dare pass a different judgment from both of these?'

Heads turned to stare at the enkenethal, with the red ridge on his back fiercely erect and his purple ears, one horribly wounded. Few had seen one of these legendary beasts before. Their hostility fell, subdued by awe.

Voices muttered, 'THEY won't just kill her. THEY'll torture her. She'll die a terrible death anyway, but before she does, she'll tell THEM more about us and our plans than ever she meant to.'

'You're all forgetting one thing, more important than anything else.' Tom's voice, cut through the argument. 'If we take the first step in faith, if we begin the rising, if we stop behaving as if we were THEIR slaves, it will start to come true. This is what everyone's waiting for, all over the country. Like it says in the song, *One new morning our Prince will appear...*'

There was a gasp of realization all round the hall. Then hundreds of voices rose with his. *'And make his land free!'*

Honesty and Berlewen thundered out with all the rest:

'When the seeds of his kingdom sprout again,
Where will you be?'

There were tears on many faces as the song died.

'He's got to come, hasn't he?'

'He won't leave us to face this alone any longer?'

'Once he sees we're ready to die for him?'

'He is real, isn't he? He does exist?'

There were angry shouts at this. 'Of course he's real.'

'THEY think so. That's why THEY kill you, just for singing his song.'

'Then where is he?'

Tom turned his glowing eyes to look up at Selevan. 'He'll appear, when his people need him. And I'll be the first to follow him to the death.'

Selevan gripped his hand.

Berlewen, too, gripped Honesty's arm. 'But can't everyone see? It's Selevan! He's here already!'

Gawen tickled Petal's throat. The enkenethal purred.

When the wild cheering died, silver-haired Livvy spoke up again. 'Well, you seem to have agreed to risk Berlewen's life at Headquarters. But how do you propose to get word into the Dock factory to warn the slaves what to do?'

It was Honesty's turn. Shyly, nervously, she raised her thin hand. 'My brother Colan's in there. My father went to look for him, and he didn't come back either. It wouldn't look odd if I was to go there and ask about both of them. Daft maybe, but it's what happens. Families looking for their own. 'Course, it wouldn't do any good, not in the ordinary way. They'll just put me

inside, like they did my dad. But once I'm in there...
They must have found ways of passing news to each
other, mustn't they, the slaves? Once I'm in, I can tell
them whatever you want me to. And then, when you
need us to rise, you give us a signal.'

Selevan bowed to her. 'I am honoured to know two
such brave girls.' The smile blazed for them out of his
dark face. Honesty, like Berlewen, felt it pierce her to
the very core.

'What's the signal going to be, then?'

'The Prince's song!'

'Couldn't be better.'

But every rebel in the hall knew that, for Honesty and
Berlewen, it could hardly be worse.

Chapter Fourteen

A half moon had risen, casting an uncertain light over the Glastonbury meres. Some stars were reflected in the open water, but more often the half-light silvered beds of reeds and left the pools darkly shadowed. It was hard to know what was land and what water.

Berlewen shivered. Honesty glanced at the older girl anxiously. Berlewen's face was pale; she stared into the water, remembering that cavernous mouth opening in front of her. This time, they did not have the enkenethal with them.

Gawen had been detailed to pole the girls across the flooded levels to the dry land where their dangerous ways must separate. Berlewen clenched her fists and stepped into the little boat.

'You'll look after Petal for me, won't you?' Berlewen begged the one-eyed farm boy. 'I daren't take him with me. Those thugs would kill him on sight. But I feel lost without him.'

'Trust me,' Gawen promised. In the faint moonlight his mouth seemed to twitch.

'He didn't like being tied up in that shed,' Honesty remembered. 'I thought he'd bring it down round his ears, the way he was leaping about and howling.'

'Shut up!' said Berlewen. 'It was horrible saying goodbye to him.'

'Poor Prince.'

'His name's Petal.'

'He's a prince to me.'

'But the real Prince? It must be Selevan, mustn't it? When he smiled at me, I felt I was turning to jelly. I feel like Tom does. I'd follow him to the death. Why can't other people see it? Why are they still waiting for somebody else?'

Honesty turned her face away and trailed her hand in the water. 'Selevan's a war-leader. That's the sort of Prince you want, isn't it? But when I first saw him, he didn't make me feel... well, *wonderful*. And I thought the real Prince would. That's why I call the enkencthal Prince. He makes me feel wonderful!' she laughed. 'Only then... when I volunteered to go to Dock, and Selevan smiled at me... well, I know what you mean.'

Gawen whistled a tune under his breath.

'What about you, Gawen?' Honesty demanded. 'You serve Selevan. Is he the Prince?'

Gawen poled on in silence.

'Why doesn't he come out into the open and tell everyone? Claim his crown?' Berlewen burst out. 'We need the Prince *now*.'

The little boat snaked its way around islets which all looked alike to the girls, though evidently not to Gawen. Berlewen peered down at the tricksy light on the mere.

'Is this safe? She won't rise again, will She? The Ancoth?'

'We haven't got Prince – sorry, your ladyship, Petal –

with us, this time,' Honesty pointed out.

'She'll probably let you pass tonight,' Gawen said. 'You're going unarmed. Maybe She won't notice you're trying to start a war.'

'But a war for the real Prince! For freedom!'

'It's all the same to Her-From-Under. Wounds to the earth.'

'It's more like a revolution, isn't it?' said Honesty. 'For peace and justice. Not a real war. We don't want to hurt anybody, if wc can help it.'

'I do!' said Berlewen fiercely. 'I'd kill those men who hurt Petal.'

A sudden rising wave threw them sideways. Gawen lost his balance for a moment, then steadied himself and the boat with a nervous laugh.

'What was *that*?' Berlewen whispered, though she was sure she knew. 'Did She hear what I said?'

'I don't think Her-From-Under hears, exactly. She just knows in her bones.'

'I wish Petal was here!'

The incredulous howling of the tethered enkenethal still rang in the girls' ears. Petal had not been able to believe that they would leave him behind.

The surface heaved again, and slowly settled into stillness, except for the silver drops raining from Gawen's oar and the slight whisper of their wake.

'You're lucky. I think She's giving you the benefit of the doubt.

'I expect She knows you won't be able to hurt THEM, alone,' Honesty suggested. 'She might be sorry for you.'

'Sorry! … More likely She heard me talking about Petal.'

It would have been madness to bring the enkenethal, but Berlewen had not expected to feel so very cold and lonely without him so soon. She still had Gawen and Honesty with her for a little longer. It was going to get much worse.

A few minutes later low shadows barred the stars ahead. Honesty leaned forward. As the bow slid softly into the muddy shallows, she grasped the bough of a willow tree and leaped ashore. Berlewen followed more heavily, in boots that still felt sodden from the night before. She could not help expecting a great arc of grey to leap from the boat and the enkenethal to land with a drenching splash behind her. She would have to get used to being quite alone. She missed the solid feel of Map's staff in her fist.

When the boat was fast, Gawen smiled and raised his hand to them, releasing the smell of cows in the still air. 'Go in peace.'

'I didn't come for peace!' Berlewen burst out. 'It's a war for freedom.'

'Look after Prince,' said Honesty.

'Petal,' corrected Berlewen. 'He sounded as if his heart was going to burst, poor lamb.'

Gawen's one eye danced in the moonlight. 'I'll make sure that enkenethal is where he needs to be.'

It seemed an odd way of putting it.

Berlewen shouldered her knapsack. 'Headquarters is east from here? I just keep walking?'

'It hardly matters which way you walk. Once you meet THEM and show them your summons, THEY'll take you to Headquarters. Only you mustn't let THEM catch Honesty with you.'

'Am I doing the right thing, telling THEM about Glastonbury, when THEY'd stopped believing the rebels could possibly be here?'

'The rebels will leave tomorrow, in small groups. They'll only be one night's march behind Honesty.'

'Won't there be children left behind?' worried Honesty.

Gawen put his hands on her shoulders. 'Don't be afraid for us. Be careful for yourself. Peace with justice doesn't come cheap.'

He stepped back into the boat. The light craft skimmed out into the moonlight until it became just one dark shape among many black islets and there were only the silver ripples at their feet to tell them he had ever been there.

Chapter Fifteen

A cold wind blew over the chalk hills. The cheeks of the sky sagged, an exhausted grey. Berlewen tramped along in no good temper, a frown scribing dark lines between her heavy eyebrows.

'This is ridiculous. Two days since Glastonbury! Here I am, flaunting myself in broad daylight, and no one seems to want to arrest me.'

She was hungry too.

When they had parted at the edge of the Glastonbury mere, Honesty had walked west, Berlewen east. No one really knew where THEIR Headquarters were. Yet there was a feeling that it must be somewhere in the middle of England. She was up in the hills now, with only wild sheep for company. She had still not met any of THEIR forces.

Hour after hour she scanned the countryside ahead for the sight she needed, yet most feared. Her throat was gripped now, not with hunger but with sick apprehension. Fear made her irritable.

'What are THEY playing at? All I want THEM to do is arrest me and take me to Headquarters, for heaven's sake.'

A colder thought struck her. If THEY found her far from any village, alone on the hills, where she had no business to be, would THEY waste time questioning her? What if THEY shot her on sight and discovered the summons only when THEY checked her corpse?

She quickened her stride. She wanted now to get down off these lonely hills, to be where there were farms and people and better-trodden lanes, where she would not be such an obvious target.

She looked over her shoulder. The hills were bare of trees. Only short turf cropped by silent sheep, wild, unkempt. Last night she had knocked at a cottage door, but no one had answered. She had tried to shelter in the barn, but the dogs had chased her away. She was damp and muddy from a night spent under bushes.

She let her eye travel the grassy plateau warily, where the slow sheep moved. Her heart ached with loneliness. She admitted at last what it was she was searching for.

'Petal?' she whispered. 'I thought... Well, I know I *said* "Stay". But I hoped you wouldn't.'

It was a treacherous reproach. For her, Berlewen St Kew Trethevy, to set out to be caught by THEM deliberately was dangerous enough. She should not, must not, wish the enkenethal here. THEY knew a magnificent beast like Petal could not be ordered or controlled against his wish. He gave his loyalty where he chose. If he seemed to obey Berlewen sometimes, it was because he loved her, unlovable though she felt herself to be. That was why THEY had given orders to exterminate his sort. That was why Berlewen, Countess of Tintagel, had been out with her father hunting on Bodmin Moor and had found the shivering pup crouching in the spatter of blood and guts that had been his mother's lair.

Nothing stirred but the sheep. No flapping purple ears, no whipcord tail lashing its tassel into tangled knots, no flying ridge of red fur. Bitterly lonely, tension rising, her courage leaching away, Berlewen trudged on.

She tried to whistle the Prince's song.

'*Is* Selevan the Prince? If he's not, why are we doing all the suffering on our own? Can't the Prince see we need him *now?*'

There was a dark line appearing ahead over the edge of the plateau. She watched it rise slowly. For several seconds, Berlewen could not make sense of it. It was not a level band now, but a silhouette increasing in size. As the grating roar reached her ears, her heart lurched with uncontrollable fear. This was what she had planned, what she had been walking towards for two days. But she was terrified.

The dark grey metal-flanked vehicle lurched up the stony hill towards her. There were heads rising above its sides to stare at her. There must be at least half a dozen of them, counting the two in the cab. Guns were rapidly unslung, aimed towards her. Headlights flashed at her unnecessarily. For a moment she stood frozen. Then, remembering the daring plan she had rehearsed in her imagination so many times, she ran towards them, waving the once-white document she had snatched from her dress. She half-expected the snap and stutter of bullets, quick pain, the fall into failure, death. Yet there was no time for imagination now. She was acting.

She was still running. The hilltop was silent. The truck had stopped.

A man was leaping out of the cab. You never knew what to expect with the agents of THEM. They might be leather-clad thugs, or elegantly suited and suavely polite, yet more sinister. This one was dressed like a slighter-built version of the thug with the orange hair who had shot Petal. His bony body was sheathed in black leather trousers and singlet, gleaming like a newly-painted drainpipe. Dark glasses blanked out his eyes. Silver rings dangled from his wrists and ears.

'Well, well, well. What have we here? A long way from home, aren't we, darling? Or are you the shepherdess?'

It was unsettling not to be able to meet his eyes, when she knew he was looking at her.

The four men from the back had jumped to the ground now. They fanned out to surround her. The driver of the truck leaned forward, crossed arms resting on the steering wheel, grinning as he watched.

Berlewen drew herself up as tall as she could. She regretted the too tight gingham dress borrowed from the chambermaid, which had been quickly washed and dried for her at Glastonbury. She still had her boots, but she would have welcomed her plumed hat and velvet riding habit, marking her out as one of the nobility. That was small protection against the contempt of THEM, who amused themselves by playing this game of lords and peasants, making their helpless subjects into figures from a fairy tale. Still THEIR agents might think twice about abusing a countess, unless they had been given express orders to intimidate her.

'I am Berlewen Zenobia St Kew Trethevy,' she managed, with hardly a shake in her voice. 'Three weeks ago I received this summons to present myself at Headquarters for the Choosing. I set out, but near Glastonbury I fell in...' She had a wild impulse to laugh hysterically. If THEY knew what had happened when she physically fell in the mere... 'Did you know that there are rebels hiding on Glastonbury Tor? They took me prisoner...'

Leather-Vest's ribald laughter stopped her short. 'Rebels, on Glastonbury? Don't wind me up. You'll have to think up a better story than that, darling. You do know what lives in that mere, don't you? Of all the places in the world you *wouldn't* want to set up a camp, Glastonbury is the runaway champion. Even THEY give it a wide berth, and there's precious little THEY're scared of.'

So Tom was right. Hope shot through Berlewen. THEY *could* be made afraid. And he had told her something else. These men in the truck were not exactly THEM, only THEIR soldiers, who did THEIR dirty work.

'That's the point.' She stamped her foot. 'That's what I'm telling you. These rebels know how to get past the Ancoth... sometimes. That's what makes it the only safe... well, nearly safe... hiding-place. Where THEY can't reach them.'

The patrol looked at each other uncertainly, jaws moving, Leather-Vest's earrings swinging as he swivelled his head to query the rest.

'So how did you escape?'

'There's a causeway.' Was she giving away too much in her eagerness to sound convincing? 'I took a risk. They never guessed I would. Not once I'd seen what the monster could do. The water heaved once, when I was halfway across. I was scared out of my mind, but nothing else happened.'

'Why?' The laughter had gone from Leather-Vest's face. He took a step closer 'Why *exactly* would you want to escape from there?'

He was taller than she was. She wished he would not stand so close. She could not back away, because the ring of soldiers was closing in behind her. There was an intensity in his question which made her shiver.

What did it mean? That Leather-Vest believed that anyone who reached the rebels would want to stay there? Would he himself have wanted to?

All this in seconds. She could see nothing behind the dark glasses to reassure her. She had to answer him convincingly, and the faces of the others were changing, growls of assent rising, their mockery dangerously shifting to suspicion.

'I'm not a peasant!' she snapped. 'I don't take orders from scum. I want to go where the real power is.'

The men looked baffled now, even awed.

'You *want* to go to Headquarters?' Leather-Vest asked, almost gently.

'Why?' Her turn to sound a little uncertain. She must act it well. 'What happens at the Choosing? I thought a summons... I thought it meant you had a chance of joining THEM. If THEY chose you, of course.'

There was a burst of raucous laughter. Leather-Vest flipped her muddy hair off her shoulder and let it fall again. He walked all round her, his impenetrable stare making her feel he was stripping off her clothes, seeing through all her layers of pretence.

'Well, well, well. Berlewen, I'm-a-Noble, Sod-You, Trethevy. Is that really your name?' He snatched the summons from her. 'Got a bit smudged, hasn't it? And muddy too. Tut, tut, tut. This doesn't look properly respectful to THEM. Black mark there, I'm afraid. Berlewen... Zenobia... St Kew... Trethevy,' he read with difficulty. 'Well, you didn't make it up, after all. This is a genuine summons. Always supposing you're her.' He looked round at his patrol, who were listening cynically. 'I suppose we'd better execute it, and leave THEM to decide. Even if she is a teeny bit late.'

'Execute her? I could do with a bit of target practice!' A thickset middle-aged man stepped forward, laughing coarsely. He slung his gun round into position, fondling it. Berlewen knew little about guns. Only the forces of THEM were allowed weapons that fired. It did not look like the handgun that had shot Petal. This was bigger. It seemed to have a string of bullets looped over the stock ready for use. Too many of them.

'Shut it, Carl. I said execute the summons, not the kid. Carry it out. Obey orders. Get it?'

'Grr! Shame. I was beginning to look forward to that.' He put up his wicked-looking weapon with exaggerated regret.

Berlewen felt suddenly on the point of collapse though there had been no bullets. It was only then that she realized how extreme her terror had been.

'Get in.'

She made to climb on to the back of the truck, but, with what sounded like an oath of annoyance, Leather-Vest pulled her back by a handful of her dress and thrust her towards the cab. He jumped in beside her and the door slammed. The truck skidded round in an unnecessarily tight turn and roared back to the edge of the plateau. The blunt nose dipped downhill. A patchwork of fields and farmhouses and encroaching forest rushed up to meet Berlewen, as she was catapulted forward. Leather-Vest seized her before she could hit her head on the windscreen. The pace steadied.

Berlewen had never ridden in a motor vehicle before. She tried to hide the fact that it was more terrifying to her than a bolting horse. As frightening as the company she was in. She found herself longing to be back on Bodmin Moor, for those gallops with the feel of responsive horseflesh between her knees, hands firm on the reins connecting her to an animal who trusted her, a shared desire to storm the morning with a high heart and clear the hedge in front of them. Here in THEIR vehicle she felt she had lost control.

Chapter Sixteen

Berlewen stood hugging herself in the small windowless cell. It was taller than it was wide, making her feel dwarfed, as well as imprisoned. She had been without food or drink for so long that every last shred of confidence had drained away in weakness. Nobody had come near her. The locked handle had not rattled. Even the shutter on the tiny peephole had not been lifted for a jailer to look in on her. Had THEY forgotten she was here?

She was sure THEY had not. It was all part of THEIR contempt for everyone except themselves. THEY wanted to make her feel like nothing. Well, THEY were succeeding. She was cold, she was miserable, she was frightened. The guards had taken away the good woollen cloak Honesty's mother had given her. She had only the skimpy gingham dress.

The walls were a sickly shiny green, the floor hard smooth grey, the door solid metal. There was no warmth of wood, no woven coverings. A single light glared at her from above, brighter, crueller than any light she had known, except that night when THEY had come looking for her at Tintagel.

She started violently. There was a sound at last. That metal handle was turning. She found she was backed against the wall, shaking. With an effort, she drew herself upright and tossed her long black hair back. She was Berlewen Trethevy, Countess of Tintagel. She must not let THEM break her.

The door swung easily open. Leather-Vest stood there.

She felt a rush of relief. She had not expected it to be someone familiar. Then doubts came slithering in. Why was he looking at her like that, grinning? What did he know? What was going to happen? If only he would not wear those dark glasses, so that she could read the expression in his eyes. All she could see were twin reflections of that harsh white light.

'Well, now!' He smiled, with what might be an oily pretence of friendship. 'You're favoured. It's not the interrogation room in the basement for you… yet. THEY want to meet you.'

It was what she had wanted, but now she was terrified.

She was being hurried along a shiny corridor. The grey floor gleamed; she could almost see herself in it. Light flashed from that same unnaturally smooth substance on the doors they passed. There were strips of harsh light overhead, so bright they hurt her eyes to look at them. Nowhere was there natural stone, timber, soft flame. As a child in Cornwall, she had sometimes uncovered substances like these from the past: a faded yellow bucket, brittle with age, yet refusing to rot; a tangle of cut wires covered with something shiny which was not quite rubber. 'Plastic' her father had called them, after much scratching of his head. These must have been useful once, but were forbidden now.

But here at Headquarters, these materials were everywhere. For THEM.

Then they turned into a wider corridor, and suddenly everything changed. The clatter of their feet was silenced by thick carpets. The door ahead was more massive than all the rest, bronze-coloured, heavily studded. It occurred to her that it might indeed be solid expensive bronze.

Two sentries, in uniforms more formal than Leather-Vest's shiny trousers and singlet, guarded it. Black tailored jackets, impeccably pressed, knife-edged creases down their trousers, white gloves and shiny peaks to their caps, which shaded their eyes. A black leather-like band crossed their chests diagonally, leading to a belt with a gun discreetly in its holster. The memory of the one that had fired at Petal made her cold.

They drew themselves up to attention, identically rigid.

'Countess Berlewen Zenobia St Kew Trethevy, Countess of Tintagel, to see the Board,' Leather-Vest drawled, as though he savoured with amusement the discrepancy between the impressively rolling syllables of her name and her total lack of power.

The guards did not appear to move. The double doors did not swing open. Instead, with an inexorable slowness, they began to slide apart. A crack of light showed, more concentrated than the blue-white glare of the corridor in which she waited. She saw an expanse of carpet, grey, patterned with black. Dark green velvet curtains were draped across the further wall. A massive table, like black marble, rested on slender silvery legs. A deeply shaded light hung over it, angled so that it threw those who sat behind the table into heavy shadow, while directing its glare straight into Berlewen's eyes.

She blinked and winced away from it.

'Come in.' The voice was deep, calm, almost kind.

Berlewen stepped forward, screwing up her eyes. She wished she could see who was talking to her, but all she could make out was the impression of many heads, perhaps two dozen, seated at the table facing her and at its two ends. She had an uncertain impression that most of them were short-cropped men's heads, but she could not be sure. She felt like a rabbit frozen in terror, before that battery of stares which she could feel but not see.

The voice came from behind the point where the light was most intense.

'You are late for your summons, Berlewen Trethevy.' The tone was civil, amiable even. There was none of the bullying menace of the guards who terrorized Cornwall. But she felt ice slide through her stomach, down to her feet.

'I was captured by rebels. They took me to the island of Glastonbury.' She was pleased that she managed to hold her voice steady.

'When the summons was served on you, our representatives were attacked. By an enkenethal.'

'I couldn't stop him! You know what enkenethals are like. That's why you're exterminating them, isn't it?' Her voice faltered. She realized it was a mistake to argue with THEM.

'Yet you kept one?'

'I found him in the nest. He was only a pup. All the

rest were dead, and the mother too. Father was going to club him, but I wouldn't let him. I was only a child then.'

'A child, Berlewen Trethevy, who sounds inclined to rebellion.'

'Not against THEM!... against YOU...' She was confused. She had never before thought that she would be at Headquarters, in the presence of THEM. She did not know how she should address THEM, face to face.

She felt the others around the table staring. Some even laughed, guardedly.

'Against us? Aren't we all one people, Berlewen? Rulers and ruled. All working for the good of our country.'

She was tempted to snap at him that her parents claimed Cornwall was a separate country, and none of them wanted to be ruled by THEM. But she held her tongue.

'Aren't we, Berlewen?'

'Yes,' she muttered. Another lie. Not sufficiently convincing. 'Yes,' she said louder, trying to smile.

'We sent a correctional force, which failed to find you. So you want us to believe that you then set out to obey our summons and come to Headquarters of your own free will?'

'I knew I had to. After what my enkenethal did, I only had two choices: to wait for your troops to come back and punish me, or to come here as fast as I could.'

'And then, amazingly, you fell in with traitors.'

'I didn't even know they existed until then! As I got nearer to Glastonbury, I kept hearing stories about a horrible monster in the mere. I never dreamed there could be humans on the island.'

'You heard stories? From whom?'

Berlewen felt herself go pale. She had not meant to endanger the farmer's family in the safe house. There were laws which said that any stranger in the parish should be reported.

'Most people shut their doors when they saw me coming. But if I met someone out of doors towards nightfall, I'd show them my summons and tell them I was on my way to Headquarters so they must take me in.'

'No one has reported this. They should have done. And did these people tell you about the rebels too?'

'Not a word. I knew I had to get past that mere, but I was trying to keep to the higher ground, well away from the water. I kept imagining I was seeing the monster starting to rise. And then suddenly, they were all around me. About twenty of them, armed with knives and spears. They demanded to know everything about me, who I was, where I came from, what I was doing so far from Cornwall on my own.'

'So you showed them our summons?'

'Yes. But they didn't believe me. They decided I must be a spy for you. They said there was no other reason I'd be so near their camp, because everybody else was terrified of the monster. They took me prisoner, to Glastonbury.'

There was a cold silence.

'I do not believe you either.'

He rose. As if at a signal, all the other figures around the table stood too. The shaded light swivelled. The merciless glare left Berlewen's eyes. Now it streamed downwards on to the uncovered heads that had been watching her. It cast strange shadows down their faces, making eyes look sunk in caverns, noses like beaks, chins jutting dangerously. They were all dressed in dark, chalk-stripe suits, with neat ties knotted over white shirts. There were a few women among them, but all wore their hair cut short and the same formal attire. In the cold light, all their faces looked pale, unnatural. Berlewen shuddered. She could understand now why they were called THEM. Though some were young and others grey or balding, they bore no sense of individuality. It would be no use appealing to any one of THEM. THEY would speak with one voice. She was not even certain which one had spoken to her. She thought it was probably the taller man of the three most directly opposite her.

The light swivelled back to her. THEY were lost in sudden darkness. She was caught in the glare.

The tears of fear and disappointment that burst from her were genuine. Had she come all this way, risked so much, been terrified so often, for nothing? What would THEY do to her now?

A fragment of song wandered through her head. *One new morning...* It brought back memories of blue skies, a walled garden. She longed to hum it aloud.

A woman spoke. Berlewen blinked and squinted, but tears stung her eyes and she could not see past the light. She thought it might have been that younger one, small-built, with gleaming black hair capped close to her head, who stood near the end of the table.

'What you say is impossible. A few years ago we heard rumours there might be a nest of rebels there. I led a force to deal with them. We lost many soldiers. But not one of them was killed by a human. I believe in the

Ancoth, because I have seen it and what it can do. I do not believe in your rebels. No one can cross that mere. You are lying.'

Berlewen hesitated. How much was it safe to say?

'Your force went armed? With guns?'

'Of course. It was necessary to enforce Justice and Peace.'

'Glastonbury *is* a risky place. The rebels lose people too. The Ancoth doesn't really seem to be on anyone's side. But She particularly doesn't seem to like war, wounding the earth.'

Even as she spoke, she realized the implication of what she was saying. If the Ancoth really would not let anyone pass bent on war, how could the rebels break out to start the resistance? How could they ever bring about the great battle when the Prince would come to lead them at last?

She was beginning to despair.

A third voice cut across her thoughts. It sounded like an old man's, level, grating, like a stone drawn across slate. 'You imply that what the Council for Justice and Peace does is questionable? That we mean harm to this country?'

'Of course not! The Ancoth's just a monster, a brute. She doesn't understand what you're trying to do.'

'And what *are* we trying to do?'

The silence was appalling.

The ultimate test. She could defy THEM, longed to defy THEM. To tell THEM in ringing tones exactly what she thought of THEM. Berlewen St Kew Trethevy, standing up for freedom, truth, genuine peace, real justice. Instead, she must crawl to convince THEM, make THEM believe she truly wanted to be one of THEM, or at least be allowed to serve THEM.

'To make our country great, peaceful and free.'

She could feel the bitter taste of the words on her tongue. She wanted to wash her mouth clean. She had to stand and wait. There was a movement among the many heads behind the table. A murmur of conferring, opinions passed around the black table-top. She could distinguish nothing.

At last someone spoke from behind the light. She recognized the first man's voice.

'You're a clever girl, Berlewen Trethevy.' It sounded less like a compliment than a threat.

A shrill bell sounded behind her. When she turned, the bronze doors had slid open again. An armed guard she did not recognize marched stiffly in, clicked his heels and bowed to THEM. No word was spoken, yet he seemed to know what he had to do. He marched her away.

Chapter Seventeen

The enkenethal padded his way across a ploughed field.
Lumps of clay stuck to his enormous feet, so that each
one fell heavier than the last and it grew harder to drag
it out of the sucking earth. Rain moulded his wiry coat
around his massive rib cage. The purple ears, one half
shot away, drooped. Rivulets funnelled from them and
from his hanging snout. It seemed impossible that he
could follow her scent through this squelching
downpour.

Yet he found the bank where she had hollowed
herself a hole under the hedge, like a badger's sett. He
snuffled a heap of leaves in the heart of a beech wood,
still fragrant with her scent. His long legs covered the
ground doggedly, in a fast, if ungainly lope. It had taken
him a day to break free from the shed on Glastonbury.
But he must be catching up with her.

There were no carpets now. Rough concrete steps led
twisting down into a corridor where the lights burned
weaker. More flat metal doors, from which the clatter of
their boots echoed hollowly. A sound came ghosting
from the far end, like a shrill wind. A few steps closer,

and Berlewen recognized it as the sound of a human scream.

After the warmth of the Council room, it was very cold.

When the guard opened one of the doors, she hung back. He pushed her inside. Then it clanged shut behind her and she was alone.

It was a little larger than the cell THEY had kept her in. The walls were the same pale shiny green, the light too bright again. There was a metal table. Several black boxes were attached to it, from which wires ran to the wall. She did not want to understand what they were for. There was a single metal chair, facing her. Somehow she knew that the chair was not meant for her.

She stood waiting for a very long time.

When at last the door opened behind her, Berlewen was too frightened to turn. She felt a start of surprise when a small dark-haired woman walked past her and seated herself behind the table. Her face was pale, yellowish in this light, her mouth a slash of painted red. The sleek hair was cut into angled points above her ears. It was the woman who said she had led the force against Glastonbury.

She began to question Berlewen. There was no expression on her face or in her voice. She rested her fingers together over the table and made no notes. Occasionally she moved a knob on one of the black boxes in front of her and a green or red light flashed, like small sinister eyes. Berlewen felt she was being made to talk to this box, more than to the woman.

The questions seemed almost too good to be true. Though the woman had said she did not believe in the rebels, she questioned Berlewen closely about their plans.

There was to be a rising against an important target, which might even be Headquarters. The attack on Dock would be a diversion, to draw the forces of THEM as far away as possible. Berlewen played down the rebels' numbers.

When she had finished her story, the woman sat staring at her, saying nothing. Then she rose, produced two black wires attached to small pads. She fixed one to each of Berlewen's palms and connected the free ends to another box, set in the side of the metal table. This time the light sprang red. Berlewen flinched, expecting the pain she had been dreading, but none came. The woman repeated her last three questions. Berlewen answered as before.

She felt sweat on the side of her temples. This was not physical torture, yet. Only the hot anxiety of getting her story right. She did not know what new danger she was in.

The woman was watching a panel on the table, not Berlewen's face. When she had finished her questions, she nodded contemptuously and snapped the red light off.

'So I was right. You are lying. But why? You must know we have more persuasive methods of extracting the truth from you. But you interest us. You seem to be intelligent, an aristocrat from a privileged home. You could either have obeyed our summons immediately or tried to rebel, though you, like others, would bitterly have regretted that mistake. But why this concocted story, so very dangerous for you? What do you have to gain by telling us things that cannot be true? We can learn the reality quickly enough, once we decide to break you. But in the wreckage of your mind and body, you may not be able to tell us coherently *why* you did this.'

She rested her pointed chin on her hand and stared at Berlewen. Her dark brown eyes waited for information, but gave nothing away. Yet she seemed to soften, to offer an invitation. Berlewen found herself suddenly longing to tell her everything.

With a tremendous effort she stiffened her resolve. 'I really wanted to do something useful. For THEM... I mean, for you. I don't know what usually happens to the people who are summoned. Do they just become your guards, or slaves, or what? I hoped...' She flushed now, because it sounded even more presumptuous than when Honesty had taunted her with it. 'I wondered if one day... if I could prove myself good enough, of course... I might... become one of you.'

The woman looked genuinely startled. Then she pushed back her chair and laughed.

'So? Not only brave, but ambitious. And bold enough to say so to my face. It really might be a pity to break someone as interesting as you. We shall, of course, if there is the slightest chance that your story about a rebel camp could be true. But at Glastonbury? No!' She gave a violent shudder. 'I was there. I saw that beast rise, what it did. Your story is nonsense, but your powers of invention may prove usable. Should we ever come to trust you, the Department of Information might be a suitable destination for your talent... If you survive your basic training, of course.'

She gave no signal that Berlewen could intercept, but the door opened. This time it was Leather-Vest who came to lead her away. For all the mockery of his smile below those blanked-out eyes, she was almost glad to see him.

As they left the room, she heard the woman speaking low into one of the black boxes. 'Utter fabrication. But it might be as well to tighten security across the West Country.'

With a shock of despair Berlewen knew she had failed. THEY did not believe her story. She had only increased the danger to the rebels and thrown away her own life.

Chapter Eighteen

Leather-Vest led Berlewen along the corridor. His bare shoulder lurched against her. She flinched away, sure that the contact had not been accidental. He laughed and nudged her again.

'Well, well, well. There's a turn-up. I was sure I'd be taking you for a last walk down to the basement. How did you manage to con THEM? THEY're not stupid.' His dark glasses flashed a glance around the empty corridor, as though he might have said more than he should.

Berlewen went red. She snapped back, 'I thought *you* were THEM... I mean... us?'

He looked at her sharply, alarm in the movement. For a moment he seemed uncertain how to answer her. He stopped abruptly and pressed a small red circle in a steel-coloured panel in the wall. To Berlewen's astonishment, two shining sections slid noiselessly apart. There was a large cupboard behind. Leather-Vest stepped in, pushing her with him. She tried to struggle. It was too small. There were no windows, nothing but blank metal walls. The doors were sliding shut, walling her in with him. She beat her fists on the door, but it was solid, locked. In her panic she did not notice what Leather-Vest did, but her stomach lurched. The floor felt as if it was rising under her feet, forcing her upwards. There was another jolt and the sickening motion stopped.

The doors did not open. She felt a slow cold terror now. Was this where they tortured people? In this small sealed room? What would he do to her?

Leather-Vest put both hands hard on her shoulders. She could not escape his greater strength. He spoke rapidly, urgently. 'Shut up. We only have a few seconds.' He licked his lips, then whistled. Only one line, but the song was unmistakable.

'You!'

He put his hand over her mouth. 'No time for questions. I can see by your face THEY haven't got to you yet. Just for a moment, I thought you'd switched. Keep faith and we can make it happen. *One new morning...*'

'*Our Prince will appear.*'

For a second they smiled at each other. Berlewen blinked back a treacherous urge to burst into tears. Then he pressed a circle on the wall and the doors parted to show another corridor.

He led her in silence to a large dormitory, also windowless. The same cold shiny green walls. Naked light bulbs left no secret shadows. Their blue-white light made the room seem even colder than it was. Beside each neat grey bed there was a small metal cabinet. There were no pictures, no books, no clutter of personal trifles, no fluffy toy on a pillow. There were stark posters on the walls:

TO SERVE HERE IS A PRIVILEGE

TO COMPLAIN IS TO REBEL

IF YOU DO NOT REPORT DISLOYALTY AT ONCE YOU ARE A TRAITOR

A stout square-framed woman was coming down the aisle between the beds towards them. She wore a navy blue suit, a white shirt, black tie, stockings and shoes. She was older than the striped-suited young woman from the Council who had interrogated Berlewen. The lines round her mouth ran downwards. Her cheeks sagged, as though she had given up smiling long ago. She looked at Berlewen hard, but her expression gave nothing away.

Leather-Vest pulled himself up to attention. 'Officer Taylor, a new recruit reporting. Countess Berlewen Zenobia St...'

'Kew Trethevy,' Berlewen finished for him.

The dormitory officer pulled from her pocket a white plastic label. She slapped it on to Berlewen's wrist.

'Number 1647.' She pointed to the far end of the room. 'Shower. Put your clothes in the bin. There'll be a new uniform for you when I've shaved your head.'

Leather-Vest wheeled and left. Berlewen shot a last longing glance as he turned, desperate for the warmth of his smile, a lift of the eyebrow. His face showed nothing. He was gone. She did not even know his name. She had the heartbreaking fear that she might never see him again.

Officer Taylor led her to the shower room. Berlewen

had no idea what this could be. Rain showers only happened outdoors. As they entered, she recognized it as a sort of bathroom. There was a row of sinks. But instead of a bathtub and buckets of steaming water, poured by maids like Honesty Olds, there was a cubicle with glass-like doors and shiny pipes.

Shivering with fear as well as cold, Berlewen stripped herself under the officer's unsmiling stare. The dress Honesty had given her, her last muddy and ragged link with Tintagel, dropped into a metal bin. She knew she would never see it again. She stepped into the cubicle, then screamed as jets of cold water scoured her. She obeyed the snapped order to smear herself with soap. She was shuddering uncontrollably when she stepped out again.

The towel she was handed was grey and harsh.

'Bend over,' ordered Taylor.

She felt the razor scrape the back of her head. Long wet black ringlets tumbled into the bin in front of her. Her scalp was shaved all over, bare, cold, exposed.

There seemed nothing left of the person she had been.

The uniform had no dignity. Grey underwear. An unbelted smock of brownish slippery material. A square cap to cover her shaved head. Slippers that slopped and did not fit, making it hard to walk easily, let alone run away.

Officer Taylor thrust a cloth and bucket into her hand. 'You will scrub this shower room until there is no trace that you were ever here.'

Berlewen filled the bucket with water. She looked at the wet floor, where her feet had left smears of mud. For the first time in her life, Berlewen St Kew Trethevy got down on her hands and knees and began to scrub.

'As if I were a chambermaid,' she muttered under her breath, as Officer Taylor left the dormitory.

Her arms ached and her face was perspiring when the officer returned. She had done her best to make the floor, the sinks, the shower sparkle. She had not known that grease was so hard to shift, the way that black mould grew round the backs of taps, that if she wiped a clean floor with a muddy cloth she would have to wash it all over again. Berlewen sat back on her heels, exhausted.

'Get off your backside!' snapped the navy-suited woman. 'You jump to attention the moment you see an officer, you lazy slut.'

Berlewen held back the urge to argue. She scrambled to her feet and stood stiffly upright. Officer Taylor swivelled slowly to study the washroom. She ran her finger round the gleaming rim of sinks. She went into the shower cubicle and came out again. Finally she came to the lavatory, where Berlewen had emptied the dirty water away. As she turned round, there was a gleam of sadistic satisfaction in her eyes. She advanced towards Berlewen with unhurried deliberation. One hand, with its white cuff beneath the navy jacket, shot out and seized her collar. A knee propelled Berlewen into the cubicle. Her head was forced down towards the still-brown water. Now she could glimpse the viler dirt she had failed to notice under the rim.

'You call that *clean*? Then you can drink it!'

Berlewen retched. Her ears, her nose, her open mouth were forced under.

***

Honesty was taking a risk. The sun had not set yet, but her desperate need of speed, to reach Dock and warn the slaves of the rising, drove her out of her woodland hiding as the shadows lengthened. Farmers should be safe in their cottages by evening curfew and there was no reason for agents of THEM to be out patrolling these wet fields. But still, you never knew. She felt clumsy with tension as she crouched in the shelter of a hedge, then made a run along it for the copse ahead. She breathed more easily here, though at every step twigs seemed to crackle underfoot like gunshots.

She had her eyes on the greying sky through the branches ahead. It would soon be nightfall. Safer, but slower. She needed speed, yet it was vital that she was not caught.

Then the little noises of her progress were shattered by a crash just behind her. She screamed. As she turned in terror, a huge shape launched itself with a howl through the holly hedge, breaking it apart. The impact slammed into her shoulders, knocking her to the ground. Mud, twigs, water spouted around her. She lay helpless in the dirt, face smothered, limbs pinned painfully into the litter of leaves by a weight she could not fight against. She could have wept, not just from fear of what would happen to her now, but from unbearable disappointment.

A mottled belly, scored with bloodstains, pinned her down. Something wet was slapping her face. Huge painful gusts of breath were fanning her ears. The hairy chest that had descended on hers was heaving and panting with whines of joy.

Honesty blinked away the tears. She managed to free

one arm to reach up around the rough-coated neck.

'*Prince? You?*'

'Sorry! Sorry!' gasped the enkenethal.

As he fell off her sideways, Honesty sat up. She put both arms around him now and looked into his eyes accusingly.

'You bad animal! We left you tied up in a shed on Glastonbury. Berlewen told you to stay. What are you doing here?'

'Sorry... Couldn't let you...' he panted.

'But Berlewen went the other way. Why follow me?'

He whined and rubbed his wounded ear against her. She cuddled him closer.

'You're right. Berlewen has to get inside Headquarters. You wouldn't last long there once THEY saw you.' She shivered at the thought. 'But I have to get to Dock as fast as I can. And *secretly*.'

'I'll be very quiet,' he whispered.

She kissed his flared purple snout. 'I'm not sure you know how, you bad boy.' Then she laid her head on his warm neck. 'But oh, Prince, I'm glad you're here. I was so lonely.'

He twisted his giant head to lick her ear, panting in ecstasy.

She struggled to her feet. The enkenethal bounced up beside her. He was so tall she could rest her hand on his back without stooping.

'Come on, then. We've got to hurry. But it's dangerous where I'm going too. Somehow, I've got to get inside that factory and deliver my message. I've got to tell them the signal, so that the slaves know when to rise against THEM. I can't imagine how I'm going to do that. And you'll have to turn back there, Prince. If the guards see you, they'll shoot you.'

He lurched against her legs, twitching his rear end in what was meant to be a wag of comfort, but almost knocked her over again. He gave no other answer.

They were soon at the further edge of the copse. While they had been rapt in greeting each other, the sun had slipped below the horizon. Hanging clouds meant that darkness was coming quickly. Cautiously they stepped out into another field.

For three more nights they travelled in exhausting marches, leaving the farmlands for the uninhabited hills. When the fourth yellow dawn struggled through the mist on Dartmoor, dirtier clouds belched up to meet them, carrying a sour smell. Dock, with its weapons factory, lay directly below them.

Chapter Nineteen

Berlewen was scrubbing the front steps of Headquarters in the grey light before sunrise. It had to be done this early. It would not do for one of THEM to walk out of the grand black doors and find a skivvy on her knees with a bucket.

Headquarters was gleaming, spotless, as the castle at Tintagel with its dusty banners and cobwebby carvings could never be, no matter how hard maids like Honesty worked. Here, all the surfaces were blank, lacking in ornament, characterless. Berlewen was frightened her own character was being stripped from her, her past life blanked out. She willed herself to remember hunting on Bodmin Moor, the enkenethal bounding beside her pony, the luxury of her carved four-poster bed, with its thick eiderdown and the lavender-scented sheets Honesty had so carefully ironed.

She shivered in the dawn wind. The shapeless uniform she wore took away all self-respect. There was no belt around the colourless, shapeless overall. The square cap of floppy, slippery material hid her shaved head, where the hair was beginning to grow back itchily. The loose felt slippers wanted to fall from her feet as she knelt. Her hands were sore, her knuckles red and cracked.

The guards, on either side of the door above her, yawned as their night shift neared its end. She glanced up at them. They were both young men. How long was it since they had come in from the countryside, obeying their summons to serve THEM? It came to Berlewen with a chilly shock that most of those in THEIR service were young. The pale lack-lustre girls who shared her dormitory. The edgy young guards still learning their duties, but growing more bullying with every year they survived. What happened to them after that?

How long could she hold out? The food was poor, tasteless, watery. She was not starved, but she was always hungry. The poor diet lowered her spirit, sapped her strength. It meant that all her effort must go into completing the long day of heavy tasks, each job done faultlessly and meekly. There was no energy left over for rebellion. The slightest mistake, a hint of argument, even presuming to use a more efficient method than the one Officer Taylor's work-schedule specified, brought an inevitable beating. Taylor, the dormitory officer, administered this discipline herself. The down-turned mouth levelled at these times into the nearest she ever came to a smile. In the few days she had been here, Berlewen had suffered fourteen beatings, with a metal-tipped whip. Even the slippery overall snagged on the crusted scars of her back. She counted them over, like badges of pride, as she scrubbed harder.

But shivering in her thin uniform it was hard not to despair. She had risked so much to get here. She had told the rebels' story, as she had promised Selevan. Yet her words had trickled away into silence down the dustless corridors of Headquarters. No one believed her. Now she was THEIR slave, with no hope of escape. It had all been for nothing.

What had that woman said? *'If you survive your basic training...'* She must survive.

She glanced at the guards again. Very quietly, under the scrape of her brush and the slop of her bucket, she started to hum the Prince's song.

'Shut it!' rapped the right-hand guard.

There was a moment's hesitation. Then, as if afraid to appear less loyal to THEM than his mate, the left-hand guard shot out a foot. He kicked Berlewen down the steps, then picked up her bucket and threw it after her. They both roared with laughter. The filthy water ran from her face, drenched her uniform, flooded its grime back over the steps and trickled away into nothingness on the drive. She would have to go round to the back of the building for more and begin again, and the sun was almost rising.

Berlewen lowered her eyelids over the rage she knew was flashing in her eyes. Head bowed, she picked up the empty bucket and returned to the tap in the back yard. She had learned to walk with controlled haste in the floppy slippers, but the soaked material clung to her body. Scrubbing the front steps was only the first of her long rota of wearying tasks. Her arms ached already. If she appeared to rush, she would be beaten for carelessness, yet THEY must never see her at work. She was supposed to be invisible, worthless. Though Headquarters must be at all times perfect, no servants could take the credit for it.

Unfortunately, she was not inconspicuous enough.

There was something about Berlewen St Kew Trethevy that made it difficult not to notice her. Officer Taylor saw her refilling her bucket. She advanced upon Berlewen.

'Haven't you... finished that... by now? ... Slut!... What have you done... to your uniform?'

The rebuke was punctuated by a series of vicious blows to either side of Berlewen's head. Her ears rang. She made no attempt to defend herself or blame the guard. It would only have doubled her punishment. As it was, her fifteenth whipping was scheduled for that evening, when she would already be on her knees with tiredness.

Soaked, humiliated, sore, she still had to return to finish scrubbing the steps, and quickly now. The sky was lightening from grey to palest blue, a line of gold beginning to show above the trees that flanked the drive.

As she came round the corner, someone was standing on the wet steps in front of the guards. A small neat figure with black cropped hair. Berlewen's heart leaped with something that was both hope and fear. It was the woman who had interrogated her, the one who had been sufficiently intrigued by her story to keep her alive and not to torture her... yet. *The Department of Information might prove a suitable destination for you.*' Berlewen had imagined herself at a desk, in a suit like this woman's, perhaps even with the opportunity for subversion.

The reality was that this woman eyed from head to foot the soiled cap, the drenched overall, the flapping slippers. Berlewen felt to the core of her pride the degradation of her status, her dress, the all-too-obvious evidence of recent punishment. The woman herself was dressed with meticulous precision: chalk-striped suit, black tie, white shirt, her lips startlingly red, her high-heeled boots sharply black. The mouth smiled, a gash of colour in these stark surroundings, then she was instantly businesslike.

'You will be ready to come with me in ten minutes. We do not believe your story of rebels on Glastonbury. But although you lied to us – and we have scientific evidence that you did – it is possible that you wove a fabric of deception around a thread of truth. We intend to find out what that was.' The dark brown eyes stared into Berlewen's. There was no friendliness in them, but their steady thoughtfulness seemed almost kind, compared with Officer Taylor's sadistic malice. Berlewen felt again a dangerous urge to confide in her, but the next words warned her of her mistake. 'If you try to trick us there, the Ancoth will deal with you even more satisfactorily than the correction unit here at Headquarters... which you have yet to experience.'

She snapped her fingers. A tall shadow stepped from the half-open doorway behind her into the light. Leather-Vest's face betrayed no emotion. He did not even look in Berlewen's direction.

'Give them to her,' said the red-lipped woman. 'I do not wish to travel in the company of someone who's obviously a cleaner, let alone one as filthy as this.'

Leather-Vest's eyes were still prudently lowered. He held out a neatly folded pile of clothes to Berlewen. She could not yet see what they were, but the cloth was crisper, the colours sharper, grey and white. Her spirits rose, until she remembered the woman's warning. She was playing a dangerous game.

Just for a moment, a hand brushed hers, warm, human.

For several seconds afterwards, she stood holding the clothes, too startled to move.

'I am not accustomed to being kept waiting. Go to your dormitory and change at once. You have eight minutes left. Report back here immediately,' the woman snapped. 'Bring the vehicles round,' she ordered Leather-Vest, 'and the armed escort.'

'Right away, Officer Feng.' He saluted smartly. 'They're in the transport yard waiting for the word.'

Berlewen had turned obediently down the steps, to reach her dormitory round the back of the building.

'Go through the front door,' Officer Feng's voice chided her. 'It's quicker. If anyone challenges you, say you are obeying my order.'

Berlewen swallowed. She had been a slave at Headquarters only a few days, and yet it took an enormous effort of courage to walk up the steps and through those grand doors, clutching the new clothes to her chest. She could not shake off the terror that she would be stopped and savagely beaten. She hurried down the wide corridors, past tall closed doors, into the more familiar, depressing surroundings of the slaves' dormitory.

No one was about. The other skivvies would be hard at work. But her eyes went nervously to the door, fearing the approach of Officer Taylor.

She unfolded a grey jacket and trousers, a white shirt, and a black belt to hold the trousers securely. Exchanging her wet overall and cap for these, she felt prouder, smarter, more confident.

She had pulled on all the garments she had been given before she discovered what was missing. There were no shoes. She must put on the over-large slippers again. With a sinking heart, she realized that nothing had really changed. She was still THEIR slave.

'THEY're making sure I can't run away.'

She pulled a face, and at once looked over her shoulder to see if anyone was watching.

On her way back to the front door, she met two startled skivvies, dressed as she had been. They stared at her and flattened themselves back against the wall to let her pass. It made her feel strange.

A shock was waiting for her when she reached the door. There was not just one vehicle waiting at the foot of the steps, with Leather-Vest at the wheel and Officer Feng already beside him. A fleet of grey lorries was lined up on the drive behind it. Their open sides were bristling with armed soldiers, all staring at her, some grinning. She could not guess what Officer Feng was planning.

Feng motioned Berlewen towards the cab of the lorry immediately behind her own vehicle. Unhappily, Berlewen shuffled in her slippers down the steps towards it. The fat hairy driver leaned towards her and pushed the door further open for her. His grin was much too wide. She had to climb in beside him. She had hoped she would be riding with Leather-Vest. Now she was more scared than ever.

The bull-nosed car and the lorries began to roll down the long drive. Berlewen sat staring ahead at the back of the leading car. She held herself as far away as possible from the fat driver. The convoy reached the deserted road and swung west.

Chapter Twenty

Honesty and the enkenethal crept down off the moor into the outskirts of Dock.

The ruins towered around them, taller than granite tors, but more unstable. Windows gaped, roofs were falling in. Here and there a jagged hole had been blasted in a wall. Blackened and rotted rags of curtains quivered in some of the gaps, like dirty cobwebs.

'This must have been a great city once,' said Honesty, her hand on Prince's neck for reassurance. 'I wonder what happened to all the people.'

A shudder ran through Prince's frame.

'Yes,' said Honesty. 'That's what I think too.'

They moved deeper into the weed-grown streets, keeping in the shadow of the walls, though there was no one in sight.

Suddenly there was movement. Out of a side street, furtive shapes nosed into the wider thoroughfare ahead of them. Honesty and Prince stopped dead, rigid. Sharp muzzles, wild and ravenous eyes, ears ominously flattened, turned in their direction. A pack of wild dogs. The ridge along Prince's back bristled. Though his feet did not move, his whole body strained to meet them.

'No,' whispered Honesty. 'There are too many of them.'
The air was full of growling. Bared teeth flashed.

Prince shrugged Honesty off, like a fly from the shoulder of a carthorse. He moved one giant paw forward. With a howl, the pack swirled about and pelted back around the corner, out of sight. Prince lifted his head. His yellow eyes shone up at her with love and pride. She hugged him.

They moved on cautiously past the opening. The side street was deserted now. Prince stalked proudly beside Honesty, bumping into her knees with every other step, guarding her closely.

'You mustn't come much further,' Honesty argued. 'I want to be seen. I've got to get myself arrested. But THEY mustn't catch you.'

Prince gave a low growl and strode resolutely on. Honesty let her hand rest on his shoulders. He felt warm and comforting. She did not know how she could send him away.

'Go, boy!' She stopped and pointed back the way they had come. Prince looked at her idiotically, as if he could not understand a word.

There was no doubt which way she should go. The noise drew her. It was the only pulse of life in this ghost city. Louder and louder it beat, at the heart of the murk that was fouling the morning air. Though the rosy dawn was spreading over the moors behind them, it became darker, rather than lighter, under the sulphurous yellow cloud into which they were walking. They began to glimpse a great bay at the end of streets. Waters that should have sparkled with sunlight were stained with the same gloom.

Now sharper sounds distinguished themselves through the constant booming. The repeated clash of metal, echoing across the water and back from dark wooded shores.

Abruptly, the shelter of the streets ended. Houses had been levelled here to leave a brick-littered space. Facing them rose a blank wall, impossibly high, topped with jagged spikes. It stretched in either direction as far as Honesty could see. Over it, she glimpsed the top of a still more massive building. There were high narrow windows near the roof, which blinked like feverish eyes. Red light flared up within and was smothered again, pulsing with the pounding of the sound that was almost deafening them now. Evil-smelling smoke hung low over the open space before them, creeping chokingly across it into their lungs, making their eyes smart.

'Fancy working *inside* that! Living with that sound and smell for your whole life.' Honesty's whisper was appalled. Suddenly, her imagination took her back to Tintagel, the sunshine in the walled garden where Grandfather worked, the gorse-bright slope above, where the wind flapped her clean washing, and the bay where the wave-caps danced over the sea.

'Colan! Father! How can they stand it?' She felt ashamed and guilty that she was still free. She grasped her staff resolutely.

'Stay,' she murmured to Prince, hugging him and planting a farewell kiss on his head. 'I've got to find someone. I feel sort of invisible. I was sure some guard would have stopped us by now. I'm supposed to get myself arrested, to get inside the factory. How else can I tell the slaves what's going to happen, and how they've got to rise against THEM when they hear the signal? If I don't get on with it, the rebels will be here before I'm inside.

'But you shouldn't have come this far. Please, Prince, go away, quickly, while you still can. THEY won't arrest *you*. THEY'll shoot you. Oh, please.' Delicately, her fingers fondled the bullet wound that had torn away half of his purple ear. The scar was healing in a black ridge. 'You've got me safely here. I wouldn't have got past those wild dogs on my own. But this is it. *Go.*'

She tried to speak firmly, but the enkenethal only slobbered, 'Sorry! Sorry! Sorry!' and licked her hand enthusiastically.

She began to walk on, venturing now into the open space, with the high stone wall of the factory looming above on her right. When she looked round, to her dismay, Prince was following.

'Go back, you bad boy.'

'Sorry!' grinned the enkenethal.

It was a long exposed walk. She was sure eyes must be watching her through the yellow smoke. Why did nobody challenge her? Her nerves were strained for the sudden burst of gunfire that would put all her plans to enter the factory out of reach for ever.

She rounded the far corner of the wall at last and the scene changed. For a second, her attention was distracted from the sinister, unbroken barrier. The full extent of the bay flashed before her. A shaft of sunlight had defied the yellow-brown fog and was beaming down on it. Then the light was blotted out. The water in front of her became a dull slimy green, sliding in slickly through rectangular basins. There were grey launches, menacing shadows against the quay. They had guns mounted on them. She thought she could make out the silhouettes of patrolling guards.

Instinctively she looked around for cover. Over to her left rose a hill almost free of buildings, except for the lighthouse set up on its summit long ago. The slopes were covered in grass. Rank and soiled by the dirty air, it swept waist high, smothering the paths that had once looked out to sea.

'Halt!'

Honesty was jolted back into the dangerous present. Prince snarled. Only twenty paces away a guard was standing, feet braced apart, his weapon levelled at her.

He hasn't shot me… yet, she thought, though it was hard to breathe. Her heart was pounding in her throat.

She tried to steady herself and look at him straight. His uniform was yellowish-brown, as though the fog had solidified and taken human shape. There were flashes of red on his shoulders. He wore, unnecessarily, dark brown sunglasses and a cap with a peak low on his brow, which made it hard to read his face. The only touch of humanity showed in the cheap silvery rings that cut into the flesh of his pudgy fingers.

Beyond him, she could glimpse other brown figures, alert now, weapons raised.

'Please,' said Honesty, desperately trying to remember the script she had rehearsed, 'I've come looking for my brother and my father. I think they're in there.'

'I ask the questions!' he roared, making her jump with nerves. '*Name?*'

'Honesty Olds.' Was that wise? Would it make it worse for her family, if they were still inside? She must not let herself think that they might already be dead.

'What's that… monstrosity… you've got with you? If he snarls at me once more, I'll spatter his guts from here to Cornwall.' The barrel of the gun had shifted, more shakily, to Prince.

He doesn't realize Prince is an enkenethal, Honesty crowed to herself. He's probably never seen one, or he wouldn't wait for him to growl.

Enkenethals were a forbidden species, to be destroyed on sight.

'He's a Cornish ridgeback,' she gabbled. 'He's harmless, really. Quiet, Prince. *Friend*.'

A long shudder of distaste ran down the enkenethal's wiry coat. He said nothing.

'THEY took my brother for a slave two years ago. We think THEY brought him here. My father set out to look for him, but he didn't come back either. Are they inside? Who can I ask? My brother's called Colan and my father's Luke Olds.' She was pleading now. She had forgotten about the rebels' plot and what she was supposed to do and say. But she was doing it anyway, because she really, desperately, wanted to know if the people she loved were inside this hell.

'You don't suppose we give that sort of information? In fact, we don't give any information to trash like you.' Even behind the glasses and under the peaked cap, the face looked smug, boastful, the thick lips spreading in a triumphant sneer.

'There must be somebody higher I can ask. Where do I have to go?'

'Nowhere. Your sort don't speak to THEM.'

It wasn't working. It was ridiculous to have been so

afraid, for herself, for Prince. Nothing was happening. She wanted to shout at him, 'Aren't you going to arrest me?' She had to get inside, but she mustn't let him suspect that was what she was trying to do.

What if she rushed at him and kicked and scratched him, pretending to be out of her mind with worry? Would he arrest her then? But she looked at the squat heavy gun, which was levelled now at her abdomen, and knew she would never reach him before he mowed her down.

There was a movement behind the guard. Honesty thought for a moment that the wall itself was moving, slowly exploding inwards. In her confusion, she had not noticed that in this second length of wall, which stretched away from the corner she had rounded towards the docks, there was an enormous gate. Now she saw its huge grey panels swing apart and from it emerged a pathetically small party. Thin, ghostly pale, moving with physical weakness and cowed docility. Some were clad in shapeless, grey-brown smocks, others in the rags of the shirts and breeches they had worn when they were summoned. These rags too were soiled to that same dreary, uniform colour. Two more armed guards escorted them.

Honesty's heart leaped with both hope and distress. Surely, these must be slaves from the factory? But they were so pitiful, so worn and starved, she could not say whether she wanted to see her brother or father among them.

She started forward, tears springing to her eyes. Before she had taken a few steps, the first sentry barred her way, using his gun with both hands to block her. She scarcely registered the relief that he had not fired it yet. She strained to see past his broad shoulders.

'Colan! Father!' she shouted as hard as she could. She knew it was stupid. Why, out of all the thousands in this factory, should the people she loved be among this half dozen?

The little procession checked briefly. As they stilled, Honesty saw for the first time what they were carrying. A long, thin bundle, carelessly wrapped in dirty cloth. A bony hand had slipped through the layers and was dangling helplessly. They were carrying a corpse. And now fear overtook hope in Honesty's heart.

The sea breeze seemed to whip her shout away. No one but the sentry could have heard the names clearly. Yet one of the slaves lifted his head and turned his face towards her.

He could not be her brother. He was younger, or at least smaller. The wispy hair that the breeze lifted was fair, under the grime. His pointed face had caught the direction of her voice, but he did not seem to see her clearly. His head merely quested in her direction, as Prince's did when he stood quivering with the effort of locating a particularly exciting smell. Honesty had a sudden intuition that this small fair boy was almost blind.

Beside her, Prince gave a low howl. He seemed to have seen the corpse for the first time and started to tremble. One of the guards with the burial party heard the sound. He raised his gun.

'Hide, Prince!' shrieked Honesty.

A whirl of grey shot past her. At the same moment, the report rang out, stuttering back from the long wall in multiple echoes. Prince was gone. Only a commotion in the long grass on the hill showed his path. The guard fired again. The grass stood still.

'Prince!'

She was past the first guard, almost before she realized it. Now she stood torn. The burial party was close in front of her now. The guard still had his gun raised. Should she confront him, or race after Prince, who might be wounded, dying?

She made a split second decision. She might never have this chance again. Prince knew this was why she had come. He wanted her to go on.

She forced herself to give the guards a shaky smile. 'Please can I ask them just one question? I only want to know if my brother and father are still alive.'

It made no impression. The guards were whipping the burial party on. The first sentry was behind her now, close at her elbow.

'Get out of here!' he snapped. 'Before I change my mind. You said that ugly brute of yours was Cornish. Then take yourself back over the Tamar while you can still run.'

Her mind raced. How dangerous would it be to provoke him further? If he shot her, her message would die with her. If only she could get near enough to speak to one of the slaves.

What should I say? she asked herself. If I only get time for one sentence? Will I ask about Colan and Father, or will I tell them about the rebels' rising and the Prince's song?

What was the use of finding out that Colan and Father were still alive, if she did nothing to set them free?

She shivered. The hope she was bringing these poor weak wretches was so small and faint. How long did the rebels expect them to hold out before the gates fell? Was she bringing a message of life or death?

The burial party moved on with their burden. They staggered under the weight, though from the look of that skinny arm, the body could not be heavy.

Honesty started to follow, chattering to the first sentry as she did so, but he was growing more aggressive now. It must be the presence of the other guards, witnessing his efforts to get rid of her, which was making him nervous of appearing soft.

'I'm not telling you again. You get out of sight of here in two seconds, or I'll... *shoot that brute!'*

His startled eyes shot past Honesty. She did not have time to turn. The sentry was still bringing his gunsight to his face when she was thrust aside. A huge grey body catapulted past her. Two heavy paws slammed into the sentry's shoulders and knocked him breathless to the ground. His gun skittered away over the pavement. With a shout, one of the other guards broke from the party and started to run towards them, while the other steadied his weapon against his shoulder and took aim.

Honesty threw herself flat, as the first bullets whistled over her head and rang against the stone wall behind her. She glanced at the fallen gun, just out of the sentry's reach. She wondered if she should dive after it. But she would not know what to do with it. Guns were for THEM.

The snarling Prince had seized the sentry by the collar. He sprang away. With an enormous surge of strength he leaped for the grass-covered hill. An enkenethal at full stretch is a magnificent sight. Purple ears streamed out like banners, one long, one short and tattered. Muscles rippled under his wiry shoulders and flowed along his flanks, as though a whole pack of hounds was running under his skin. His tail flew out behind, taut as a towrope.

One of the guards swivelled. A vicious stutter of bullets raised spurts of grit in the wake of the flying beast, but the great strength of the enkenethal tugged the winded sentry with him, like a sack of hay. Black boots drummed on the ground. His face was red where the collar was choking him in the grip of Prince's yellow teeth. But he hung like a sandbag defence along the enkenethal's flank, between him and the bullets. The guards might still have killed their colleague without mercy, if they could have kept up with the racing target.

A second guard faltered in his rush towards Honesty. He switched direction. Now he was chasing after Prince, stumbling on the greasy cobbles at the water's edge, in a vain pursuit of his helpless comrade and the outrageous culprit. Honesty scrambled to her feet, ignoring grazed palms and knees. The more distant guards could not see her through the fog. They were firing blindly. She threw a frantic look at the huge blank gates that had clanged shut after the burial party came out. Surely someone else would hear the gunshots and come bursting out?

The slaves had set down their load with weary arms. They were whispering nervously to each other. Could they be wondering if they had the time, the speed, the courage to escape? But none of them ran. All at once Honesty saw what she must do, why the enkenethal had gone suddenly beserk. She did not need to be captured now, to get her message inside. Prince had given her an opportunity she could never have dreamed of.

She raced forward. The fearful slaves stopped whispering and drew back when they saw her running towards them. They seemed almost as scared of her as of their guards. Only the half-blind boy stood, head cocked, listening to her swift footsteps with a little smile on his tired face.

'Listen!' she said, astonished to hear the authority in her voice, though most of these young men were older than her. 'Don't interrupt. We may only have seconds.' The other guard was still straining to catch the leaping Prince in his gunsight. 'There are rebels on Glastonbury. They're planning a revolution, and it's going to start here. They need the guns you make in the factory. But they can't break in unless you help them. Spread the word, right through the factory. When you hear someone outside singing the Prince's song, rise up. Overthrow your masters. At least keep them busy fighting you off till we set you free.'

She paused, out of breath. Some faces stared at her blankly. In others, a light was beginning to shine.

'The Prince? You mean he's coming at last? Here!'

Now joy was spreading to all their exhausted faces. Only the half-blind boy was attending to her with quiet interest. One eye wandered, sightless, milky. The other, intensely green, with a huge black pupil, seemed to regard her with more than physical sight.

'I don't know who the real Prince is,' she confessed. 'But he must come, mustn't he? If we all rise in his name, he'll appear and lead us. Be ready.'

'Run,' said the half-blind boy quietly.

No one else had noticed it. Behind them, the gates were already swinging ominously open. As the armoured tank rolled out of the gateway, with its long gun questing, Honesty fled round the corner of the wall.

Chapter Twenty-One

The burial party staggered into the barrack room in the evening twilight. Heads turned to greet them in a wave of relief that turned instantly to alarm. They had been missing for hours. The word had gone muttering through the factory that they must have dug their own graves as well. The reality those who waited saw was almost as awful. Even in this dim light the bloodstains showed as darker streaks. They could hardly walk. Pain and exhaustion screamed with every movement.

Colan and Luke forgot their own weariness to leap forward and catch Gonesek. The boy's face was like a piebald pony, ashen pale, distorted by black bruises. His blind eye rolled dully. One vicious wound had slashed across his face. The intelligent green eye was lost under the crimson swelling. His lip was split and teeth were missing.

They lowered him tenderly on to the concrete floor. Colan laid his hands gently on the wounds, wishing with all his heart that they had the power to comfort which Gonesek's hands seemed to give others.

'Why?' murmured Luke. 'What happened?'

The green eye struggled to open. The split and

swollen lips moved in a half smile. Colan bent his head to catch the ghost of a whisper.

'Do you have… a sister… with a voice… like a skylark? I think… when she stood close… there were freckles on her nose.'

'Honesty!' Father and son looked at each other in amazement.

'Friend to… an enkenethal? That's why they… beat us.' The voice was failing. 'He was… very… brave.' Gonesek fainted.

All through the overcrowded room the story was filtering in bits and pieces. Soon the air was thrilling to one repeated phrase. 'The Prince's song!'

Luke looked round, suddenly wary. He could see excitement, desperate hope, but fear too, calculated caution. He gripped Colan's wrist.

'This is too dangerous. It only needs one coward who thinks he can save his own skin by reporting this to THEM.'

'What would THEY do?'

His father shrugged. 'How can people like us guess? THEY're not like normal human beings, are they? All that matters to THEM is power, and how to hang on to it. THEY could eliminate the lot of us. Wipe the slate clean and start with a new batch of slaves who'd never heard a whisper of the Prince's song.'

'Does everyone here know it?'

'I shouldn't think so.'

'Then…'

'We'll have to teach it to them.'

'But you said it was too dangerous. If you set yourself up as leader, the Prince's representative…' Colan's heart

161

was filled with a desperate fear for his father and a swelling of enormous pride.

'I'm dying anyway.' Luke's hand descended on his son's wrist. 'No, don't argue. We both know it's true. I want to do one thing I can be proud of before I go.'

'*Dad!*' It was impossible to say everything that was in Colan's heart. He blinked back the tears and tried to smile. 'You won't be alone. I'll teach them too, and if... you don't make it... I'll carry on.' An expression of incredulity was spreading over his face. 'Honesty was here? Outside the gates? With a message from the rebels?'

Luke gave his tired smile. 'You're remarkable children.'

'I wonder where we get it from,' Colan smiled in reply.

'People are going to get hurt,' Luke warned him. 'And not just those who'll fight. Gonesek was just there at the wrong time... or the right time, for us. I don't think he'd approve of what we're going to do, even though he carried Honesty's message.'

'Wouldn't he? But he must! He must want us to be free.'

Beside them, Gonesek moaned. Luke and Colan immediately bent over him. Words stumbled through his damaged mouth.

'Don't... kill them. The guards... They don't understand... what they're doing. Promise...' His face went slack.

'We don't want to kill them,' Colan argued, as if Gonesek could still hear him. 'We only want to be free. But if they try and stop us...'

'And they will.'

Colan turned back to his father. 'You said somebody out of all this lot would betray us. But from the look of it, six of them have already been tortured for hours. Why let them go now? Does that mean somebody's spilt the beans?'

'Then there may not be much time. Let's not waste any of it.'

Above the hubbub of rumour, argument, excitement, Luke Olds' voice rose with something of its former strength. *'One new morning our Prince will appear.'*

Colan's tenor, still not quite steady, joined in with him, *'And make his land free.'*

From all over the packed room, other voices joined in, not shouting the song dangerously loud, but with quiet intensity.

'When the seeds of his kingdom sprout again,
Where will you be?'

Soon the whole room was catching the words, growing more confident each time they sang them, hope rising.

There were yells from the guards coming closer, fists pounded on the doors. Obscene oaths commanded them to be silent. The song was hushed. The men looked at each other with a renewal of fear. They held their breath. The door stayed closed; the boots tramped away.

'Listen!' Luke Olds held up his hand.

Outside, night had fallen. Yet the stillness was not quite silent. Out of the darkness music was still floating. Fainter voices were singing the same song, further away. The men listened in rapt silence. It was coming from the windows of the women's barracks.

Colan murmured to Luke, 'No one's said what happened to Honesty. Do you suppose they've got her too?'

Chapter Twenty-Two

Berlewen could see the top of Glastonbury Tor before they came in sight of the shimmering water which surrounded it. The tower on its summit, misty blue in the distance, pointed to heaven like a prayer.

Berlewen didn't know what to pray for. That the rebels would still be safe on their island? That they would be halfway to Dock, in their rash, brave bid to free the prisoners and claim the guns which THEY forged to terrorize everyone? What if Feng's army, armed with those guns, caught the rebels, equipped only with spears and bows, before then?

The soldiers behind her on the back of the lorry whistled and sang. Their songs were coarse, all about victory and killing. They laughed too loudly. The words would have been sickening, even if it were animals they were going to hunt.

They grew quieter when the convoy left the hard road. Soon they were dipping down over ever softer cart tracks, towards the mere. The air grew mistier. Berlewen could no longer see the tower rising clear of it. They must be very near the marsh now.

The edge of the water came suddenly into view, much

closer than the soldiers had realized. The belligerent songs fell silent, the last defiant words trailing away into uncertainty.

Berlewen gripped the sides of her seat. The air was cold, damp, the visibility limited to fifty paces. The soldiers were afraid of the marsh, but she had more reason to fear it than them. Most of these men had only heard rumours of the monster. They probably did not have enough imagination to envisage the word 'Ancoth' made flesh, in all its awesome horror. Berlewen had seen Her, felt Her breath, smelt the stench of the underworld, known herself helpless before Her gaze.

Yet she had survived. Why was she shaking, then? Berlewen St Kew Trethevy had gone into the very jaws of the Ancoth and lived. How would these shuddering men react if she told them that?

She said nothing. Better to be Number 1647, the cleaner, who was only here because she knew the lie of the land. Wiser not to let them understand that she was the heroic Countess of Tintagel, who battled against underwater dragons and conquered them.

Idiot! You'd have been mincemeat in her digestive system if you'd been on your own. It was only Petal's love for you that saved you.

Tears stung her eyes. Where was Petal now? There on the island in the mist, still waiting for her? Or had he set out with the rebels, marching to war, about to get himself shot in some enthusiastic bout of heroic lunacy?

Someone was opening the side door of the cab. Leather-Vest motioned her out. 'Feng wants to speak to you.'

Not a flicker of a smile betrayed him. She walked past him, stiff-faced too.

Feng stood turned away from her, on the last high bank before the grass sloped down to disappear under the still water. A few half-wild cows had galloped away from the noise of the engines, then stopped to browse again as the sound died. They were misty outlines, not far away. The sound of their jaws tearing grass was unnaturally loud. The wet of mud and grass seeped through Berlewen's felt slippers.

'Where did you cross?' The little woman swung round. Her dark eyes were very sharp, holding Berlewen's. It was difficult not to tell the truth, dangerous also to drop her eyes and appear to fumble for words.

'There's a causeway.' Surely that was safe? She needn't say the rebels also had boats, that they could land anywhere.

'Show me.'

'I… It may be hard to find. We were coming from a different direction.'

'*We?*'

Berlewen felt the blood drain from her face, leaving her dizzy. She had not mentioned Honesty before.

'I had my… dog… with me.'

'It was not a dog. It was your enkenethal. Do not lie to me. We submitted the hairs we found on your clothes to chemical examination. You know we have a programme to exterminate enkenethals.'

Berlewen did drop her eyes then. 'I never meant to bring him to Headquarters. He followed me from Cornwall. I had to leave him on the island when I escaped.'

166

'I should imagine an enkenethal would be difficult to restrain, even on the Isle of Glastonbury. Surely he would have tried to break out and follow you? Well, I suppose the Ancoth got him, like so many others.'

Berlewen said nothing. This woman did not know that her enkenethal had made the Ancoth change Her mind.

'The causeway?' prompted Feng.

'It's difficult. Everything looks different in the mist. But I think it must be further that way.'

'They didn't blindfold you?'

'No. I don't suppose they thought I'd dare to escape.'

There were rapid, low orders. One section of the troops took up station where they had parked, at the foot of the track, yet high enough to see out over the water if the mist should lift. Feng's voice rose slightly. 'Blow a whistle at once if you see anything move. *Anything*. Do you understand?'

'Yes, ma'am.'

'You bet!'

They were scared, all of them. Even Feng.

The other vehicles set out behind the officer and Berlewen, churning slowly across the soft pastures as the two of them walked around the rim of the lake.

Berlewen tried not to think about what lay under the surface. She was examining every bush and clump of trees, trying to remember just how the willows had looked on that morning when she and Honesty had stepped out in faith to follow an underwater road.

'I think…' She went down to the water's edge, where hooves had ploughed the mud. Odd that the animals were not scared of the Ancoth, as humans were. Did the hoofprints disguise the start of a human path? She took off her muddy slippers and paddled out a little, feeling each step under the cloudy surface.

'Sorry. I thought this might have been it.'

Did she want to find it? Should she tell Feng if she did? This was not what the rebels had planned. But, in a way, it would help, wouldn't it? If THEIR attention, and part of THEIR forces, were here they could not also be at Dock when the rebels reached it and the slaves rose… if they did. If Honesty had got inside with her message.

The rebels must be on the march by now. They would travel secretly by night, in small bands to avoid detection. Selevan would be leading them. She thought of the tall man with the gaunt, noble face, and her heart turned over as she remembered how he had smiled at her. Selevan was the Prince. She knew it. On the day he led them into battle, everyone else would see it too.

Would there be anyone left on Glastonbury? The children? A few of the women? Was that farm boy Gawen, with his one brown eye, still with them, left behind to look after the cows? What would happen if she betrayed them?

If Feng tried to cross the causeway, surely the Ancoth would stop THEM? Berlewen's heart jumped. Perhaps this was her high destiny, her service to the Prince, to sacrifice her life leading the army of THEM to destruction.

She paddled on along the water's edge, holding her slippers.

'Ow!' she yelled, as her toe stubbed a log.

'Well?' demanded Feng. 'Have you found it?'

Berlewen rolled up the grey trousers and explored deeper. There was more wood, logs laid in a corrugated pathway. It was no use pretending. Feng had only to order one of the soldiers to check what she said.

'I think this is it.'

The woman looked over her shoulder. There were hundreds of troops behind her, out of their vehicles now, all heavily armed. Berlewen was trapped between two kinds of death.

'How many dissidents were there on Glastonbury?'

'I didn't count. A hundred or so, I should think. But lots of them are children.' She wanted to make them sound less dangerous, to protect them. Perhaps Feng would decide that THEY had been right all these years, that it wasn't worth the risk of trying to cross.

The officer took a small grey instrument out of her jacket pocket and spoke rapidly into it. With a sinking heart, Berlewen knew now that what the rebels had told her was true. THEY could talk to each other over vast distances. Probably Feng was even now reporting to Headquarters. She might be calling up reinforcements, helicopters, bombs, anything.

'Yes, sir. Understood.' Feng folded in the tall wand on the instrument and put it away. 'Right,' she snapped at Berlewen. 'You go first.' Her face was very pale. The red lipstick showed like an ugly wound. For a moment, Berlewen forgot her own horror of what was in front of her, in the satisfaction of discovering that Officer Feng was terrified too.

'What do you…?' She tried to play for time. In spite of her dreams of heroism, she had never really expected that THEY would order Feng to cross on foot. Not after the last time, when THEIR powerful boats, THEIR flying things, THEIR long-range weapons had fallen to the horror in the marsh.

Berlewen's story had changed things. Feng's lie-machine had told THEM to believe that she had crossed the marsh on foot. Now Feng and her soldiers were being made to test the truth of it.

'Trooper Jude will be right behind you, with his gun at your back. There had better be no trickery.'

Berlewen turned and saw the fat driver of her lorry. The unpleasant grin had been wiped from his face. He was sweating.

'I shall be following both of you. If I give an order, you will obey it instantly. Do you understand?'

'Yes, ma'am.'

'Then walk. The rest of you, line up.'

The soldiers on the bank looked more frightened than ever. Feng separated out a group to remain on the shore, guarding their line of retreat. They appeared mightily relieved. The rest were muttering. Berlewen wondered if they were on the edge of mutiny. What would Feng do then? Some tried their boots in the water, testing the depth, and pulled back quickly. Those furthest away from Officer Feng were giving overloud cries of pretended terror, to disguise real fear. Feng only had to turn in their direction. Her look quenched the horseplay.

Feng gave an order to Leather-Vest, who barked it out. The troop lined up in a column. Instantly, they were a disciplined fighting force again.

Still Berlewen hesitated. She had no idea what was going to happen when she walked out on to the causeway a second time. When she and Honesty had tried to cross, they had been safe until she had left the path and ventured out into the marsh after Petal. She would not stray from it this time, but nor did she have the enkenethal with her. Instead, there was an army of heavily armed soldiers of THEM, and the Ancoth was the implacable enemy of those who threatened the peace of the earth.

The barrel of Jude's gun prodded her spine. 'You heard what the lady said. Walk!'

Chapter Twenty-Three

Berlewen splashed forward.

A few steps behind Jude she could hear Leather-Vest talking now. She had assumed at first it must be Feng speaking into her instrument. Fragments of his words floated clear before the mist muffled them again.

'... check our position... crossing to Glastonbury... no sign yet of alien creature... Trainee 1647... route-finding... Superintendent Feng will eliminate possibility that dissidents... Hello! Hello!... Can you hear me, HQ?'

Berlewen could not resist a twist of her head. The barrel of Jude's gun jabbed painfully between her shoulder blades.

'Keep walking.'

It had been Jude's face, not Leather-Vest's, she had seen clearly. Sweat was pouring from it, though the misty air was cool. She felt a sudden absurd surge of superiority. Yes, she was terrified, but not quite as much as these hardened soldiers. Awful beyond belief as the Ancoth was, Berlewen knew that it was still possible to survive an encounter with Her. The men knew of only one outcome – death. Only iron discipline drove them on.

Beyond Jude's fearful face she had had a momentary glimpse of Leather-Vest and Feng, a careful distance behind them. Leather-Vest was holding a talking-instrument like Feng's, but now he was shaking it, putting it again to his ear. Something was wrong. Even the machines THEY used to impose THEIR terror were not, it seemed, completely reliable.

'Halt!' came Feng's sharp order.

The noise of splashing boots, of timbers creaking underfoot, died away into the silence of the misty mere. Out of sight, a curlew called, a mournful lonely wail. A chill crept up from the marsh.

'The signal's cut off.' Berlewen could hear Leather-Vest more clearly now. 'I can't raise HQ.'

Jude had turned too to see what was happening. They watched Feng take out her own instrument. She pressed a key and held the machine to her ear. Like Leather-Vest, she shook it, tapped again at its keys, adjusted its retractable wand.

'Some sort of radio blackout?' Leather-Vest asked.

The officer looked around slowly. She seemed to be needing time to make a decision. A column of unwilling soldiers was looking to her for leadership. She spoke abruptly.

'We're in the shadow of the Tor. Once we've stormed it, we can climb to higher ground and restore the signal. March on.'

Berlewen took four more steps, feeling for the slippery timbers underwater. She paused to steady her balance.

The mist shuddered in front of her. She knew, even before she saw, what it was. She opened her mouth to scream, but, as in a nightmare, no sound would come. She could see nothing clearly. A wall of mud was heaving higher and higher. Water was streaming off it. She did not want to look at the scales of murky green it was beginning to reveal.

Other yells behind her rent the air. The prodding of Jude's gun in her back ceased suddenly. She was aware of the barrel swinging past her shoulder, shaking wildly.

Taller and taller the thing was looming over THEM. Berlewen dared not lift her head and meet those eyes.

There was a violent click of metal. She tensed herself for the explosive report close to her ear.

Nothing.

Further back along the line of soldiers she could hear a ragged succession of clicks. There was no accompanying sound of gunfire. The first cries of alarm were breaking up into a gabble of voices, a rising chaos of terror.

'Order!' screamed Feng. 'Company, take aim. Steady. Fire!'

More clatter of unresponsive triggers. The yells grew hysterical.

And still the Ancoth was rising. Berlewen had not fully known before the breadth of these shoulders, vast enough to bear dragon's wings, the shadow of Her neck lunging out over them.

'The guns won't work!'

'It's coming for us!'

'It's witchcraft. Kill the girl! Throw her to it!'

Berlewen turned with shock and saw their distorted faces staring past her. As she spun back to know what they were seeing now, the whole marsh erupted, shattering the fog. Far above her was the gigantic head of the Ancoth, veiled in dripping mud. Eyes flared hugely golden between curtains of weed, the only light in this cold brown marsh. Any silly sense of superiority drained away in an instant. She was as terrified as any of them. From an awesome height the eyes stared down at her. At any moment those jaws would open.

The eyes held hers. Their brilliance began to change, dwindling from gold to deep green, like moss in shadow. Darker and darker, until they were tunnels that seemed to suck her down into the heart of nothingness. She thought she was going to lose consciousness.

The mountain was sinking now. Deeper and deeper. Was She going, without breaking this terrible silence? All the men's screams were held suspended as She slowly plunged out of sight. Down and down, dragging the surface of the marsh with Her. A huge hollow was spreading out towards them, all the water of the mere pouring into it. The causeway of logs was uncovered, slick with mud. The world was tilting.

It seemed as though Berlewen must topple into that dark vortex. It would swallow them all.

Then the muddy surface heaved, so that she was almost flung sideways. Silver barred the brown. The lake came spilling back, flooding around her legs, threatening to wash her from the foothold and carry her away to a more ordinary death. But she was still standing.

It had all happened in a terrible silence. Now the shouts from the column behind were rising frantically again. There were wild splashes. From the distance of the sounds, Berlewen knew without turning that many of the men must be flailing back for the shore, defying Feng's orders.

'Halt!' yelled the little Superintendent uselessly. Then, realizing the futility, 'Company! Retreat in good order.'

They were slipping and slithering back. The men were running as fast as they could on the treacherous surface of the causeway. Some fell with a splash, scrabbling onwards on all fours. Berlewen was running too, the slimy water dragging at her ankles, like hands intent on holding her back. In front of her, Jude dropped his gun in the mud and did not stop to rescue it.

Those who had been at the rear of the column were on firm land again, most racing for the lorries. Some halted, shuddering, to wait for Feng's orders. They were torn between terror of the Ancoth and the ingrained fear of THEM.

There were new shouts from the vehicles, as the drivers struggled to bring their engines to life. A jolt, a rattle of machinery, a dry spluttering cough of cogs. Nothing happened. No roar of diesel. No metal monster sprang to life to challenge the marsh serpent. The lorries were dead, useless. Some of the men started to sob.

One of them shouted out the same word as before.

'It's witchcraft! *She's* doing it.'

Their faces, distorted with terror, were swinging in Berlewen's direction. Some instinctively levelled their guns, before they remembered they had lost their power to fire.

'She woke the monster.'

'She's in league with it.'

'Kill her!'

They were starting to move towards her, but warily. Incredulously, Berlewen realized they were afraid of her too. But their fear was breeding hatred, destroying reason. They were starting to run at her now. She backed further out into the water.

Feng stepped in front of the angry rush. 'Halt!'

Her little fists were clenched at her sides. She was smaller than Berlewen, but she faced the maddened troop, her face whiter than ever, the scarlet mouth ugly with strain.

'No one will touch the girl. If you're right... If she is part of this... conspiracy... witchcraft, you call it... the worst thing you could do is kill her. She may be the only key we have to restore normal functioning to our equipment. I am holding her as a hostage.'

'Normal functioning!' bellowed a bull-faced guard. 'She summons up that evil monstrosity, that could swallow the lot of us before breakfast, and you talk about "normal functioning"? She's a witch!'

'The Supreme Council for Justice and Peace does not believe in witchcraft. But if Trainee 1647 is indeed a conspirator, she will know how this thing has interfered with our technology, secrets which it would be very useful for us to discover.'

Feng turned slowly towards Berlewen, who was still standing knee-deep in water. She had mastered her own fear for the moment, so that her concentrated glare once more had the power to make Berlewen tremble. The girl was sick and shaking anyway. She had thought she could experience no more terror than she had known just now, gazing into those enormous eyes that were threatening to suck her down into darkness. There was no safety for her anywhere – not in the marsh, nor among the fear-crazed guards, nor now with Feng, whose brain seemed to be rapidly calculating how best to make her yield up information she did not have.

I'm alive. She tried to hang on to that reassurance. For the second time, the Ancoth didn't destroy me.

Leather-Vest came forward. He was pale himself, splashed from head to foot with mud. His voice shook a little.

'Permission to speak, ma'am?' Feng nodded. 'Trainee 1647 is, as the Supreme Council rightly says, not a witch, but an unarmed young female. Whatever links she may or may not have had with that thing in the marsh, I don't think she can pose much threat to us on land. I volunteer to have her handcuffed to me, and I'll make myself personally responsible for her behaviour.'

He did not look at Berlewen. His eyes, behind the dark glasses, were steady on Feng. She hesitated only a moment, then nodded. Leather-Vest strode down into the water. Berlewen did not resist. A steel band snapped around her wrist, another around Leather-Vest's. They were locked together. He allowed himself a brief grin, as he led her up out of the water.

'Now, madam, let's see what you can do.'

Feng was struggling to come to grips with her unprecedented helplessness and the wake of physical shock. 'I knew it! Whatever the lie detector said, I had more faith in the reality of that monster than in her story about rebels on Glastonbury. We've proved it is impossible. If it hadn't been for the speed of my reactions, we'd all have been dead meat like the others.'

178

Berlewen felt Leather-Vest's fingers twitch against hers. 'Glastonbury was nothing but a distraction. *Wasn't it?*' Her hand struck Berlewen unexpectedly across the cheek. 'The other Council members were suspicious of your tale of a rising in Dock. That didn't seem possible. Security at the armaments factory is absolute. But that doesn't mean dissidents wouldn't be foolish enough to try to attack it. Before we lost radio contact, reports were beginning to come in of some suspicious activity in the south-west. Evidence of movements at night. Patrols have begun to make the first arrests. *This* was the diversion, not Dock, wasn't it?'

The second smack brought tears to Berlewen's eyes. She hoped her sob was non-committal.

'Start all vehicles!'

Again the starters ground. The lorries stood inert.

'Then push them, you idiots!' screamed Feng, suddenly losing her composure. 'Push them till we are out of range of this cursed marsh. Push them all the way to Dock if you have to!'

The men leaped to the order that would get them away from the marsh. They ran to put their shoulders to the lorries, humping them forward over the slippery grass. It was a huge effort up the soft sloping rise, back to the firmer surface of the track.

Berlewen walked chained with Leather-Vest in a careful silence. At the top of the bank, she turned to look behind her. The mere was lost below in the mist. What had happened when that dark deep vortex opened like a terrible mouth? She had dreaded that, without Petal's help, the monster would swallow her without mercy. Instead, as the light died in Her magnificent eyes and She sank beneath the marsh, the Ancoth had swallowed the power of THEIR technology.

How far from Glastonbury would the soldiers drag Berlewen, in soggy felt slippers too big for her, before they were out of reach of the Ancoth and THEIR terrible power returned?

Chapter Twenty-Four

Honesty moved furtively from corner to corner of the narrow empty streets. She was in an older part of the city now, down by the waterside. At the end of a lane she glimpsed one of THEIR grey-painted patrol boats against the quay, and drew back swiftly. The pursuit from the factory had fallen away behind her, but surely ahead the city must have an outer ring of sentries, which she had somehow slipped through unchallenged earlier that morning.

If it was still morning. The air was, if anything, growing darker. At first, she had been too shaken and breathless in her panicked flight to wonder why. Then, as she slowed and steadied herself, she assumed the evil-smelling brown clouds must lie heavier down here, blocking out the light. She saw now that this was not true. The murk was thinning. The air smelt a little cleaner, a whiff of seaweed came from the harbour. Wisps of fog trailed past. Beyond, the abandoned buildings stood out sharper-edged. But not for long. They were dimming, even as she watched. It was the light from above which was fading.

It was making a darkness in her heart.

She had a second fear as she neared each corner. What if a pack of wild dogs was lurking in that next alley, waiting for a victim, fresh meat?

'Prince?' she murmured, pleading. 'Why don't you come? What's happened to you?'

She thought of the guns snapping death after his leaping figure. Had another bullet hit him? Was he lying in the long grass of that hill, his precious blood draining away into the polluted earth? She wanted him as never before. She was so lonely. Afraid for herself, afraid for him.

How long before the rebels from Glastonbury got here? If they did. If the forces of THEM didn't intercept and slaughter the little force before they crossed Dartmoor.

She came to a river, flowing out into the harbour. The water was a strange chalky green. But it would guide her. It was time she turned inland, sought the greater safety of the moors, tried to make contact with Selevan's troop to tell them she had delivered their message. Neither she nor they had planned for this. They had assumed she would be inside the factory by now.

There was a wide highway beside the river, but Honesty avoided it. It did not look overgrown. There were fresh marks on its surface, tracks like the tanks she and Berlewen had dodged on the moor. She kept under the shelter of a concrete wall that separated her from the road.

She had not gone far before the sound she had been dreading shocked her and set her pulses racing. The roar of an engine approaching. Though she could only be seen by someone looking directly down over the wall, she darted sideways, in through the broken window of a deserted house. She crouched below the sill, waiting for the noise that spelled THEIR power to pass by.

As it got closer, there was something irregular about the sound of the engine. It stuttered and then surged again, died completely and revived. She did not understand the way these machines worked, yet the sounds made her think of a sick animal, staggering with failing strength to rejoin its flock.

It limped near enough for her to hear human voices, shouting and cursing.

Curiosity overcame caution. She raised her head stealthily to peer over the corner of the window frame.

She could look down on the road from here. It was still empty. Then she saw where the uncertain engine noise and the shouts were coming from. One of THEIR boats was cutting like the grey shadow of a shark down the chalky green river. There were some half dozen men and women on board. They wore the same brown uniforms as the factory guards.

As she watched, the engine cut out again. A man in the stern was wrestling with the controls. This time the silence was not broken by a new surge of power. A woman yelled. The boat was drifting in the current, faster and faster, beginning to spin out of control. A few seconds more and it had passed out of Honesty's sight. She heard a brief roar, then silence again. Something was badly wrong.

As the stillness lengthened, Honesty slipped out to continue her flight. It had grown darker while she was in the house.

She crept on, in fear and loneliness. Dock had been a

name of dread for her family as long as Honesty could remember. The great weapons factory from which no one returned. She had expected massive defences, vigilant checkpoints, barbed wire, frequent patrols. Yet beyond the factory itself there was only this awful emptiness, a ghost city.

Could it be possible that THEIR forces were not as large as people believed? What if the terror had loomed larger than the reality?

Into her heart came a defiant hope. If we keep faith with each other, she told herself stubbornly, if the Prince comes, perhaps we can win.

But how was she to keep faith with Selevan and his rebels, when she did not know where they would try to slip secretly into the city?

And why was the day getting darker, though by her reckoning it should be about noon? She looked up, past the gaping roofs from which slates had slipped, and found the sun at last. A dull orange disc in a sky that was strangely grey though there were no clouds. She was getting colder too. It was not just the after-effects of shock. She looked up at the sun again. It was no brighter than a yellow harvest moon. Then the reality hit her. How could she stare at the noonday sun and not be blinded? She could not deny her fear now. The sun was losing its strength.

To comfort herself, Honesty started to sing the Prince's song, as she scrambled on, away from the harbour, up streets that led towards the moors. *'One new morning...'*

If the sun was dying, would there ever be another morning?

***

As Colan pushed the gun barrel he had bored along to Gonesek, he wiped the sweat from his eyes. It had become a movement of habit. He would have been whipped for stopping, even for a second, in the middle of drilling. He was so weary that only the edges of his mind realized that his aching hand had come away from his forehead almost dry. He picked up the next rod and plunged it into the cold water. He usually had to steel himself against wincing at the touch of hot metal, even through the callouses on his hands. Yet something was different. The steel was hardly more than warm. It did not hiss when it touched the water. The end was jagged.

Colan looked swiftly to his right. The man who cut the lengths of metal for the barrels was evidently struggling. Instead of the swift chop through glowing steel, he was having to force the blade backwards and forwards. The metal was cooling too fast, hardening.

It was dangerous to look around. The overseer with the whip was never far behind him. Colan lifted his eyes just enough to look around the workshop without turning his head. It took a little while to identify what was different. He drew a quick breath. Then his head was bent again, concentrating on his work, while he tried to examine the memory of what he had seen.

He glanced up again, swiftly. Yes! That was it. He could see across the vast armaments workshop, almost to the opposite wall. The air was clearer. The yellowish fog was thinning to a fainter cloudiness, paled by shafts of weak light reaching through the high windows. It was eerily beautiful.

He was not the only one to notice that something was

185

changing. More heads were turning. Even the overseers momentarily forgot to snap their whips, as they too stared at what was happening.

All the furnaces in the rows between the workbenches seemed to be dwindling. Their huge red mouths had belched out white-hot steel to sizzle and scorch and solidify into instruments of death. Now the fires themselves were dying. The blazing volcanoes were shrinking, the ovens blackening around them. The air was cooling.

The overseers were yelling at the stokers. Frantically the slaves shovelled up piles of coal and flung them into the furnaces' jaws. It only made the fire-pit blacker. The red glow disappeared, walled in by the coal that would not catch fire, smothered, extinguished.

Lashes rained down on the stokers' backs. Some fell, howling with pain, and were kicked aside. More workers were dragged from other jobs at the benches, forced to pound the bellows in a desperate effort to breathe life into the dead fires. All down the vast shed the same thing was happening.

The overseer nearest Colan was sweating from something other than scorching heat. He had started to shake with tension, even with fear.

Even the most brutal of overseers could not insist that the rest went on working. There was no red-hot metal rushing towards the anvils, no blowtorch flames for the soldering, no soda solution boiling in the vats. Production had stopped.

Slaves furthest from the furnaces were craning to see what was happening. Colan risked a glance in the other direction. At the far end of the shed, his father stood at his inspection bench, where no more finished barrels came rattling past. Luke Olds' weary face was lit with a smile.

Alarm bells rang. Colan was suddenly aware of guards posted at all the doors.

Chapter Twenty-Five

An animal howled. Fear gripped Honesty as the sound multiplied.

The street fell silent again. Perhaps it was weariness that made her slog on uphill and not turn back. Or a dispirited feeling that whichever way she took would be as dangerous as this. She reached the corner of the side street. The wild dogs were there. They were not looking in her direction. The pack sat in a circle around their leader. All their muzzles were pointing at the darkening sky, their mouths open in harrowing howls. I am right to be frightened, Honesty thought. Even the animals know something is very wrong.

The dogs did not even turn their heads to watch her pass.

Now there was greenery above her. The houses were thinning out, showing a tangle of waist-high weeds and young trees. For a country girl, it was a relief to be back in sight of natural colour, leaving behind the grime of THEIR factory and the ruined buildings. She could crawl in under those branches and rest while she thought what to do.

She turned into the short road leading to a field and

saw at once that she had been wrong. Half-hidden among the trees was a church with a square tower. This was not a field but an overgrown churchyard.

She stopped at the corner, as she had so often on the climb up, and looked back longingly.

'Prince?' How loudly was it safe to call? She tried to whistle, but she was out of breath. The long hill stretched below her. Nothing moved.

She had been so sure the enkenethal would find her. His purple snout, nostrils flaring like a dragon, would pick up her scent and track her through this hostile city. She would hear a sudden bounding of gigantic paws, feel the slam of his heavy body against her chest, his tongue slobbering over her face with enthusiasm, probably an ecstatic cry of 'Sorry! Sorry!' She loved him so much. She wanted him now.

But a last look showed her the streets were empty. And the sky was emptying with every step. For some time now, it had become so nearly dark that she had expected the fires of night to start pricking through the twilight. Yet no stars shone. As the sun's disc hung above her, almost lifeless, the fear of what was happening became more awful.

Once more she pursed her lips to whistle the Prince's song, as she made her way past the last houses towards the churchyard gate at the end of the road. She was half afraid that someone else would hear her, half hoping they would.

The thin notes of the first line died away. The silence was too huge.

A voice sent her diving for cover into the nearest doorway.

'And make his land free.'

Honesty started with a different shock. It was not THEM. Could there be people still living in this crumbling city? The Prince's friends? Or was it...?

She sang the third line, in a voice that sounded daringly loud. *'When the seeds of his kingdom sprout again.'*

The voice answered. *'Where will you be?'*

It ended in a burst of laughter. Round the corner of the next house came a familiar figure, carrying in each hand a goatskin bag dripping with water. A black patch sat rakishly over one eye. The other brown eye twinkled.

'Gawen!'

'Who else were you expecting?'

Honesty almost threw herself at him. It was so wonderful not to be alone.

'I thought you'd be on Glastonbury looking after the cows. Where's Selevan?'

'Waiting for his lunch.' Gawen shook the water-filled skins, showering drops over both of them. 'If you're lucky, there'll be enough cheese to go round. You'll find him under that apple tree.'

He led her through the gate, pushing it open with his hip. She peered ahead. In the dim air, with the branches of trees sweeping low to the long grass, it was hard to see who might be hiding in the shadows. But the trees were small. They could not be sheltering all the rebels from Glastonbury. Perhaps there were more inside the church.

She started, as a sentry she had not even noticed in the church porch waved Gawen past. But he stepped forward when he saw Honesty, barring her way.

'Who's this?'

'Honesty Olds.' Gawen turned with a grin. 'The maid from Cornwall. You must remember her.' The bright brown eye winked at Honesty. 'The girl who went ahead to warn the slaves in the factory?'

It was the sentry's turn to look startled. 'You didn't get through?'

'Oh, yes, she did.' Gawen's smile was warm.

'What are you waiting for, then? Take her to Selevan. He could do with some good news.'

Honesty ducked under the branches. She was suddenly face to face with Selevan, much closer than she was prepared for. The tall rebel leader sat under the tree, his back against its slender trunk, his hands locked around his knees. The expression in his long face was dark, even in the shadows. There were others around him, Tom, his second-in-command, and others Honesty recognized. They were slumped on the ground, as if dispirited. Selevan's head lifted slowly to meet the newcomers. His expression changed.

'Honesty!' he said, in that deep thrilling voice. 'I did not hope to see you again, unless it was… afterwards.'

'Nor did I. But I delivered your message. Really!' It was so important that Selevan should not think she had failed him. 'It didn't turn out like we expected. I met a burial party of slaves coming out, and I told them the signal. Then… there was some shooting… and I ran.' She had an aching vision of the enkenethal bounding away in another direction. Why didn't he come?

'The slaves know our plan, the Prince's song?' A blaze was burning in Selevan's eyes. He rose, stooping under the boughs. 'Well done!'

Honesty's heart turned somersaults of joy. Then Selevan stared out at the noontime twilight of the field and sighed. 'Poor souls! You gave them hope, and what have I to offer them now? A dozen of us, against all the might of THEM.'

'But the others are coming too, aren't they? Hundreds of you from Glastonbury? Won't they meet you here?'

Tom's voice came from the shadows behind his leader. 'That was the plan. Of course, we knew that some groups might not make it. None of us would stand a chance if we ran into one of THEIR patrols. But not a single other group has arrived yet. I can't understand it.'

'I am getting more afraid with every minute,' said Selevan, with his back to them. 'We crossed the marsh first, but the other groups should have been close behind us. They had orders to fan out after they'd reached the shore and take different routes, converging here. The first ones should surely have got through by now.'

Tom's rougher voice cut in. 'And something odd's happening to the daylight. While we've been waiting, I've been watching the sun climb higher, and yet it seems to be getting weaker, not stronger.'

'I know,' shivered Honesty. 'It scares me.'

Selevan still had his back turned. 'If something doesn't change soon, I fear there may be no hope for any of us.'

His solemn tone chilled Honesty. Selevan was their leader. They were all looking to him for hope. Might he even, if Berlewen was right, be the Prince?

He turned and fixed his dark eyes on her. They blazed suddenly through the shadows of his face. 'And yet, I do have hope. When the Prince sits on his throne at last, the whole world will be made new, and the sun will shine on this land for ever. Do you believe that, Honesty?'

Yes. But where is... who is...? The words would not quite shape themselves on Honesty's lips. Selevan was gazing into her eyes. A shiver ran down her spine. It was really true, wasn't it? Selevan was the Prince they had all been expecting for so long. He was asking her to have faith in him, no matter how bleak things looked. To go into a seemingly hopeless battle in his name. To die for him.

'Yes! What do you want me to do?' she heard herself saying.

'You gave our promise to the slaves. However few we are, we must not fail them. At dawn tomorrow, we march on the factory.'

'But there's a huge wall, massive gates!' Then there came into her mind THEIR crippled boat, adrift in the current. 'Only, I think there's something wrong with THEIR machines, as well as the sun. They don't seem to be working like they used to. Maybe we *can* do it!'

Selevan bent towards her. His dark eyes flashed in that rare smile that made her heart turn cartwheels. 'Well done, Honesty Olds. Not only honest, but brave. The Prince is deeply in your debt.'

He turned towards Tom, leaving her dizzy. She would do anything for him.

Gawen was cutting hunks of bread and paring out rations of cheese. She went to help him serve the others.

'How dangerous is Dock?' Tom was saying. 'Won't there be armed patrols? Electric fences that kill you if you touch them? Mines that blow you to pieces if you step on them?'

'*We* got through safely,' Honesty said shyly, handing him his lunch. 'All the way to the factory.'

'We?' Tom said sharply. 'I thought you went on your own?'

'I did. Only Prince... the enkenethal... he came after me...' She rounded on Gawen. 'How did he get out? I thought you were going to keep him safe on Glastonbury. You knew we were terrified he'd follow Berlewen if he escaped.'

The brown eye returned her stare solemnly. The black patch sat secretively over the other. 'And he didn't, did he?'

'He did! You let him get out.'

'Not to follow *Berlewen*. Would you like a drink?'

He poured water from the goatskin for her, while she stood open-mouthed.

There was a stir of activity, new voices at the gate, low, urgent. The whole group jumped to their feet, shaking the overhanging branches, scattering crumbs and upsetting water. Honesty pressed forward with the others, trying to see over Tom's shoulder. Newcomers came pushing towards them between the tombstones.

Their voices were louder now, trying to speak coherently through panic.

'The Ancoth!'

'Her-From-Under... She...'

'She rose.' This last was a woman's voice, flat, shocked out of all emotion. 'As high as Glastonbury Tor itself. There was nothing they could do.'

'It was horrible!' A man's voice now, gabbling. 'She didn't even do anything at first. I was sure She'd open her mouth and belch out fire or eat us up, or something. But She just… looked at us.'

'And then all She did was sink down. Down and down and down. And the whole marsh sank with her. I thought a hole was opening up right through to the middle of the earth.'

'The groups were spread out, right across the causeway. Ours was almost over to dry land. Then the marsh turned upside down. It threw me flat in the mud. I could feel myself slipping sideways, rolling downhill. We were all of us going down into that pit. Sucked under. But I grabbed hold of a willow and clung on for dear life. And slowly, the earth started to come right way up. The water came rushing back in this huge wave, sweeping across where that hole had been. It tore me away from my tree and threw me clear up on the shore. When I came to and looked round, there was just Livvy here, and the few you can see.'

'And the rest?' Selevan's voice rang hollow.

'Gone,' said Livvy, without expression. Honesty recognized her now as the silver-haired rebel leader who had argued against this plan. 'Swallowed under. All those brave souls who set out to fight for freedom.'

'All of them? You're the only survivors? You're sure of this?'

'Yours was the only group ahead of ours. There may have been a few still waiting to set out from Glastonbury. But I doubt if they'd put a foot on the causeway, after seeing what they did. It was dusk, but there was still enough light to see most of the way back to the Tor. There was nobody left between us and the island.'

'Why? Why?' Tom struck his fist against his head. 'Why did She rise against us? We're not like THEM. I know She hates war. But we're fighting for freedom and justice.'

'That's what THEY say,' murmured Gawen, so that only Honesty heard.

'But we mean it!' Honesty hissed back.

'It doesn't make any difference to Her-From-Under. THEM or us, the earth is still wounded.'

'Are you on Her side? Think how all those poor people suffered!'

His hands were busy, gathering up the remnants of food and drink for the newcomers. His one eye was grave. 'It is not what I want. But this may be the way the earth is made. The way *She* was made. Suffering breeds more suffering. Somebody has to break the cycle.'

'But you've come here to fight, haven't you? To set the slaves free?'

He looked at her almost angrily. 'I shall be there.'

Chapter Twenty-Six

When the sun, exhausted, slid below the western hills, they wondered if it would ever rise again. The twenty rebels slept uneasily in the church, on narrow wooden pews over a cold stone floor. Honesty saw even in her dreams the window showing St Michael slaying the dragon, dimly outlined against the last of the light.

The next dawn came, but it was no more than a sickly yellowish paling of the rim of the sky. The smoke that had always hung over Dock was thinning. In its place was a twilight more sinister still. The rebels armed themselves with spears and shields and bows. Honesty grasped her staff. They stood staring down at the city, where the armaments factory was almost lost in the gloom.

'Ready?' said Selevan.

'Aye, sir!' Tom and Livvy brought their little troops to attention.

Outside the shelter of the trees in the cool of the morning, Selevan stood tall. A sword was buckled on his hip. He held a long spear in his hand. There was a leather shield with a metal boss on his arm, a crested helmet on his head.

'He *looks* like the Prince!' whispered Honesty to Gawen.

Selevan beckoned her forward. He pointed to a bundle of weapons stacked against a tree.

'Are you with us, Honesty Olds?'

'To the death!' she breathed.

'Then arm yourself.'

She laid the staff Map had given her down in the long grass and selected a spear. It felt strange in hands that were more used to a broom.

Selevan's still face broke into that heart-stopping smile. 'Then it is time to go. May God fight with us!'

Selevan, Tom and Livvy split their forces into three small groups. They exchanged handclasps. Then each slipped away down different side streets. They would not see each other again until they met outside the factory walls.

Honesty looked round to find Gawen bringing up the rear of Selevan's troop. She struggled for a moment to see what was different about him. While others carried weapons and shields, he was burdened with a heavy knapsack.

'Your spear!' she said. 'Where's your weapon!'

There was weariness in his voice, even an edge of anger. 'I'll need both hands for the wounded.'

'But we've got to win the battle first! There are so few of us!'

'You do your job and I'll do mine.'

She felt a wave of resentment. They were so few! The Prince needed every warrior he could get. Gawen might only be a cowherd, but he was stronger than she was, and even she was going to fight. There was nothing wrong with him, except for the loss of one eye.

'Coward!'

She turned away from him and fixed her eyes on Selevan. The rebel captain was leading his heroic little band down through the streets of Dock, out of the quiet church to the noise and terror of the weapons factory, to the stronghold of THEM. The spear in her hand committed her now from the safety of that churchyard into the near-certainty of death. One thing might save them. Had Honesty given the slaves inside the courage and hope to do for themselves what these few rebels outside could not? Would they throw off their own chains, break open the doors from inside? Would they rise to the Prince's song?

They slipped from corner to corner, down side alleys, checking each opening before darting on. As the streets levelled out, Honesty's glances were searching for something other than sentries. Her heart ached still to see a majestic grey beast, his mutilated purple ear pricked, his golden eyes shining out of the gloom.

The closeness of Selevan in front of her was a comfort. Now that the years of waiting were over, there was something boyish in his eyes this morning. He ran as lightly as the teenagers, his head thrown back proudly, holding himself tall. She longed to tell him how much she loved him, that she would die beside him.

The sight of the empty no-man's-land surrounding the factory stopped them dead. There was no more shelter. And there were guards. Where only a huge deserted wall had confronted Honesty and Prince on this north side, now there were sentries spaced out at regular intervals. Brown uniformed figures, getting harder to distinguish in the murk as the distance increased. They were not vigilant enough. There was no cry of alarm as the rebels halted breathlessly in the shadows of the last houses.

Something else had changed. Where were the flashes of angry firelight, the pounding din, the rolling smoke?

Blood was pounding in Honesty's throat. To her left and right, the two other groups must be pausing to check like this. A sound from any of them might startle this too-quiet morning into yells, gunfire. In a few seconds, it could all be over.

Selevan motioned her over to him and murmured in her ear. 'You say there's no gate in this north wall? Just the one to the east?'

'Yes,' she whispered back. 'I don't know about the west side. I only saw that one gate.'

'So much the better. We want the slaves to throw the right one open.'

With a slight beckoning of his hand, he led the little group cautiously back into a side street, out of sight of the wall. They ran, lightly, silently along it. Honesty was terrified that at any moment they would meet a patrol, too soon. The spear felt unfamiliar, awkward in her hand. She looked round. Gawen was running behind her, weighed down by his knapsack. She supposed it must be full of bandages, medicines, It seemed an enormous quantity for twenty rebels. She despised him for not carrying a weapon.

When she looked in front of her again, she was unprepared for the sudden sight of a grassy hill rearing in front of her, its green shocking after miles of dirty stone. A searing pain went through her. This was where

Prince had disappeared, pursued by gunfire.

No time to dwell on that. The east gate was in sight now and the sentries thick today.

'They seem to be expecting us.' Selevan's murmur was almost proud.

Crouching at the corner, Honesty caught a slight flicker of movement. Tom raised his hand on their left, Livvy beyond. All three groups crept forward, converging on the wider street that opened nearest to the gate.

A sentry stiffened.

Before he had time to shout the alarm, Selevan burst out into the open space, singing at the top of his magnificent baritone voice. *'One new morning our Prince will appear...'*

Gulls flew up from the harbour, shrieking above the clatter of white wings. The blank walls of the factory gave back the echoes from twenty throats. *'And make his land free!'*

Chapter Twenty-Seven

Inside the darkening factory, the guards' air of triumphant brutality had gone. They were scared. And so more dangerous than ever.

A lash descended on Colan's shoulders. The whip-end drew blood from his cheek.

'Take that grin off your face. You'll all pay for this, you treacherous scum.'

But the blow had not been as sure and accurate as Colan had feared. The boy stood still, watchful. He was slowly beginning to take in the astonishing change which was making the overseers so afraid. The extinguishing of one furnace would have been alarming enough. But *all* of them, at the same time?

There was something more. He looked down the long lines of slaves, all alert to see what would happen next. Colan was suddenly struck by the difference in them. Usually cowed heads were up now, backs straightened, dull eyes coming alive with curiosity. Something else was changing. It was the beginning of hope.

From far outside came the faintest thread of sound.

There was a moment's silence, save for that thin

haunting tune. Then across the shed, a slave started to whistle the same Prince's song.

The nearest overseer yelled, 'Shut it!' and the whip cracked.

It was the half-blind boy Gonesek who fell, blood streaming from his face, lost to Colan's sight among the benches. But all around him, others were leaping to his side, fists drumming on the metal workbenches, hammers pounding on anvils. Everyone was whistling now. Then Colan broke into song and hundreds took up the chorus.

'One new morning our Prince will appear,
And make his land free.'

There were not enough overseers to silence them all. Slaves and slave-masters were battling now for control of the whips. Even the debilitated bodies of the workers could overwhelm with sheer numbers the burly well-fed men they wrestled with.

Out of the corner of his eye, Colan saw a door guard raise his rifle. His heart dropped sickeningly. They had been mad. They should have known there was no way any rising could succeed against THEM. They were all about to be massacred where they stood. He tensed for the explosion, for the first screams, the falling bodies.

There was nothing. He watched the guard's convulsive jerking, as he tried to fire again and again. Still there was only the roar and panting of the hand-to-hand riot all around him. At every guarded door the same thing was happening.

Colan leaped on to the table. 'The Prince is coming!' he yelled. 'Everything's changed. THEY're losing THEIR power!'

Then he vaulted down on the other side and ran to save Gonesek from being trampled under the feet of his friends.

Honesty dashed forward. She truly believed they would all be killed in those first seconds. She wanted to die beside Selevan, even throwing her own body in front of his, but she could not keep up with the trained rebels.

Slowly it began to dawn on her that Selevan was still upright and running, and so was she. They were all running. There was no blood, no falling bodies. Across the narrowing space in front of them, the alarm of the sentries was turning to panic. Rifles and sub-machine guns clicked uselessly. The most athletic of the sprinting rebels were on them now. The patrols bellowed for help.

'When the seeds of his kingdom sprout again...' the rebels sang as the spears went in.

Now there was blood.

Honesty had no idea how to use her spear. A moment later, it was wrestled out of her hand. She was grappling face to face with a sweating soldier. He was twice her weight, but as she dodged and twisted, she saw in a triumphant flash that, in spite of their uniforms, these men were unused to fighting. No one had ever stood up to them. They were heavy swaggering bullies. All the same, he gave a sudden wrench that nearly broke her arm.

Suddenly, his weight sagged, almost pulling her down with him. He dropped at her feet, blood spurting from his mouth. From behind him, Selevan's sword had pierced through his chest.

The rebel leader pulled his weapon out, wiped the blood on the soldier's uniform and smiled at her. She radiated back her adoration. He had saved her life.

They both started. From inside the gate another tumult was rising. Snatches of song broke through a cacophony of yelling.

'Listen! You did it, Honesty! They've heard the signal. They're rising against THEM!' Selevan's joy lit up his face.

'The soldiers' guns?' gasped Honesty. 'Why aren't they working? What's happening?'

'The heavens are on our side. Fire is dying. THEIR guns, the sun.' He cast a glance at the feeble disc climbing the eastern sky. It scarcely made a difference between dusk and morning.

Honesty longed to rejoice with him, but the sight made her afraid. If the sun died, what life could there be for any of them?

'The gates!' She had to be practical. 'We've got to open the gates.'

'We've nothing to ram them with and we're still outnumbered. The slaves will do it from inside. They'll seize the keys...'

He broke off and whirled round. Two bulls of men came charging towards them. Yet these guards had not been equipped for hand-to-hand fighting. They had relied totally on their possession of guns. The rebels were buoyed up, as the defenders fell before their swords and spears. Blood was making the ground slippery around the gate.

But the odds were turning. More guards, hearing the noise, pounded round the corner. Some of the rebels began to go down, weapons wrenched out of their grasp and turned against them. Honesty snatched up her spear. She was fighting for her life in earnest now. She had almost forgotten about her father and Colan inside.

'Why don't they come out?' she heard Selevan grunt close by. 'There are thousands of them and no guns to hold them off now.'

No guns. The words penetrated Honesty's brain. Wasn't that why they were storming this factory? Not just to free the slaves, but to equip themselves with firearms for the real war against THEM? She glanced quickly at Selevan to see whether he had realized that the guns inside would no longer help them, but he was fighting too grimly for her to tell.

The surviving rebels could not hold out much longer. Tom and Livvy were pulling their groups back closer to Selevan in front of the gate. If only it would open and a thousand slaves, however weak, pour out to help them.

Colan fought for the door. He and Gonesek were being carried forward in a great mass of heaving cheering bodies.

'The Prince! The Prince!'

'He's come at last!'

The brutal overseers went down before them, overwhelmed by the press of desperate slaves. Colan tried to avoid trampling the bodies, as he was pushed over them.

Suddenly the gloomy hall was split by a shaft of light. It was not bright, merely a glimmer striping the pall of brown. But it brought a cheer that shook the walls. The slender column widened rapidly, as the guards gave way and the outer doors of the armaments shed were forced open.

The slaves erupted into the yard, like a cask of fermented cider exploding. Scum and froth, thought Colan wryly. That's what we've been reduced to. We'll just trickle away over the stones and be dried up in the sun.

The sun? He squinted skywards, wanting to take in great visions of freedom. There seemed to be no clouds over the yard, yet the sky was a lustreless grey, rather than blue. The sun, if that really was the sun, hung, a dull orange disc, as if fogged by dust. It took the edge off the joy he should be feeling.

'Where's the Prince?'

The mob had lost direction, slowed. They had expected their saviour on a battle-charger, at the head of his victorious army.

'The gates?' Gonesek's voice murmured beside Colan. 'Are the gates open?'

'No.' Colan looked down at the smaller boy, who was turning his almost blind face up to the sky, as though he too wanted to feel the sun on his eyes.

'Get the keys!' Shouts were coming from the front of the crowd.

There was more fighting as the press of people in front of Colan struggled towards freedom. Their way was still barred by the solid gates and the jagged-topped wall. It was cold in its shadow.

The gates trembled, shook, bowed inwards. Slaves fought to get clear of the massive leaves as they were dragged open. Colan drew in a deep gulp of air. Freedom? At last!

He looked round desperately for his father. What if Luke Olds had gone down in the fighting? Not now, with the end in sight! He tried not to let himself think that his father was so weak he might have fallen under the push of bodies and been trampled by the slaves themselves. Frantically Colan searched the faces around him. The crowd was too thick. He was hemmed in. He could not see his father.

All at once, the way opened before him. Colan screwed up his eyes, though this strange morning light was little more than twilight. It was the vastness of the view that dazzled him. The bay with its rim of hills, the open sea, the yellowish sky, doubled by its reflection in the water. He had forgotten the world was so big.

Then he was through the gate and pitchforked into a scene of combat. There were so many soldiers in brown uniform that it was hard to see whom they were fighting against. A group shifted. Colan caught sight of a princely helmet, a noble figure wielding a sword amid a welter of attackers. Beside him fought a girl, in the sort of shirt and breeches he used to wear himself.

'Honesty!' his voice rang with sudden strength.

She looked round, but only for a moment. To his horror, he saw that her life was in real danger.

The wave of slaves surged forward with him. The only weapons they had were the hammers and tongs they had seized from their workbenches, but there were hundreds of them. They grabbed the uniforms from behind, pulled the wearers to the ground, stamped on them, obliterated them. It hardly needed the blades of the few surviving exhausted rebels.

'Honesty!' Colan cried again. He was at her side, hugging her.

'Father? Where is he? Is he alive?'

'He was when the rebellion began. I don't know. I can't see him.'

They both turned their heads, searching frantically.

'Look out!'

There were more guards, rushing round the southern corner. They checked, took in the size of the mob, then turned and ran, striking out wildly at their pursuers with their rifles. They were racing for the waterside, leaping into boats, pushing off, only to find to their dismay that the engines would not start. The boats swung wildly in the dark pools, as furious slaves leaped into the water after them and struggled to overturn them.

Everyone had their backs to the steep streets leading down to the harbour.

'For Justice and Peace! Cut them down! Charge!'

Honesty and Colan whirled round, as a woman's ringing command cut the air behind them.

Chapter Twenty-Eight

Feng had forced her swearing, sweating troops to push the lorries towards Dock. Time and again she assured them that they must soon pass beyond the power of the Ancoth. The engines would leap into obedient life, communications would be restored, the machinery of THEM would have back its weapons of oppression.

It did not happen. At last they abandoned the vehicles, though they still clutched their silent guns. They marched on. Berlewen's feet were raw, her slippers disintegrating.

The soldiers' boots echoed up a hill on the outskirts of the empty city. Jude, who had prodded Berlewen into the marsh, frowned up at the fading sky. 'Shine, you beggar,' he muttered, 'or we're all dead.'

They crested the hill, and bitter shouts broke out. Below them lay the sullen sea and the grim factory. But Berlewen stared down at the scene with a shock of hope. The gates stood wide open. Even in this gloom she could see the scatter of brown uniformed figures lying on the ground. A mob surrounded them, spilling out now over the open space below the factory walls.

Hope quickly turned to alarm. They looked like a

cloud of ghosts emptying out of the underworld. Ragged, half-starved, confused, feeble from lack of nourishment and overwork.

'Charge!' Feng yelled.

Berlewen turned to see the army from Headquarters, fleshy faces lowered under their helmets, powerful bodies tensed for action, break into a run. Blood-curdling yells burst from them. They had fixed bayonets to the guns that would not fire. They were terrified of the Ancoth, frightened at the dying sun. But they knew what to do with human enemies.

'They'll kill the slaves!' said Berlewen wildly, tugging at the handcuffs which still bound her to Leather-Vest. 'Where are the rebels? What's gone wrong?'

'How about there?' Leather-Vest pointed. 'Recognize the one in the fancy helmet?'

'That's Selevan! He's come! And Honesty! And I think that one's Tom. But where are the rest? There should be hundreds. Feng's lot will slaughter them! What are we going to *do*?'

Leather-Vest slipped his hand into his breast pocket and produced a key. The handcuffs fell apart.

'Stay out of this. I've got a helmet and a flak jacket.'

'I'm coming with you.'

He did not argue, but he flung the helmet at her as they raced after Feng's charging troop.

The rebels and the slaves all turned at the murderous roar from hundreds of trained soldiers charging. These were not swaggering sentries, relying on the terror of THEM to scare intruders off. This was the elite guard of the Supreme Council, disciplined fighters, at the peak of fitness.

At the expressions of ferocity under those grey helmets, the slaves fell back in panic. Only a handful of rebels, gripping spears and swords, was left around Selevan.

Berlewen raced after the soldiers. She had no idea what she could do to avert the tragedy. She saw Feng mount a hillock of rubble which commanded the battle. Berlewen crept up behind it and crouched, unseen.

The slaves tired quickly. Many fell from sheer exhaustion. Hobnailed boots trampled over their bodies, uncaring. Those who were still on their feet looked up with new horror as Feng's army darkened the already twilit air. The crowd swayed and staggered and began to run, limping and stumbling.

'The Prince's people! To me!' Selevan shouted. 'Hold fast!' Tall and commanding, he brandished his sword over his helmet plumes. The light in his eyes blazed. Though death must be the certain outcome, he would not yield.

Honesty and Colan looked at each other, then raced towards him.

There were so many fallen bodies on the ground, rebels, sentries, but mostly slaves, who had known only minutes of freedom. It was hard to sprint across the battlefield and not tumble over them.

It was Honesty, not her half-starved brother, who tripped first. Her foot caught under the elbow of a man who lay sprawled on the stones. She was down on her hands and knees over his body. She was aware of Colan, gasping for breath, but poised between her, Selevan and the charging soldiers.

'Help Selevan!' she called. 'Don't wait for me.'

The body of the slave she had stumbled over groaned. In spite of her panic she looked down, and saw him properly for the first time. His face was half hidden, his forehead bruised from the fall. Something about the grey stubble of his hair, the set of his cheekbones, though now more hollow than she had ever seen them, tugged at her memory.

'*Father!*' she whispered, as though he and she were alone in the world and not seconds away from a murderous army. Then, 'Colan!' she shouted. 'Help me!'

Colan turned. His startled gasp told that he recognized their father.

'What shall we do?' pleaded Honesty. 'We have to help Selevan. But I can't leave Father.' She threw an agonized look at the charging line of grey-uniformed soldiers bearing down on the rebels.

Colan glanced too. 'We're too late to save them.'

'But the Prince!'

'Choose life.'

He seized Luke's shoulders. With a panicky glance at Selevan, Honesty grabbed her father's legs. They seemed to have no more flesh than peeled sticks. Without a further word, they started to run with him, out of the battle.

It took a superhuman effort for Colan, in his weakened state, to carry even so slight a weight. He could not spare the strength to see where he was going. It was difficult enough finding a path through the bodies, though the casualties were thinning out as they neared the edge of the cleared ground. It was Honesty who steered them, scanning the way ahead. She worked her grip higher up her father's frame so that she could bear more of his weight, trying to spare Colan. She must not look round and see what had happened to Selevan.

'That hill,' she nodded, between gulps of air.

The long grass would shelter Luke. They stumbled up into it and fell with him, rather than setting him down gently. For a while they lay panting, too exhausted to move.

Honesty raised her head first. 'Got to get back... help Selevan... You stay with him.'

Colan levered himself on to his knees and parted the grass to look down at the battlefield. The line of charging soldiers was almost on the last knot of rebels. Feng, a small commanding figure in flak jacket and helmet, was standing on a pile of rubble, urging them on.

'Who's that?' Colan pointed a little way behind Feng.

Honesty had half risen, about to dash back into the hopeless fight. She stared. Someone was creeping up on the commander. Not a soldier or a ragged slave. The grey trousers and white shirt made her look like one of THEM. Something metal dangled from her hand. It was not a bayonet or a knife, more like a looped chain.

'Berlewen?' gasped Honesty.

Colan shot a look sideways at his sister, then at the girl's swift crouching run. 'Our countess? With THEM?'

'No.' Honesty grabbed his arm. 'Look!'

The metal chain looped through the air, one end still firmly in Berlewen's grasp. The other ring caught Feng a blow on the side of the head. The little woman spun half round, then tumbled forward. Berlewen sprang.

***

214

A moment later, she was standing up where Feng had stood, struggling into Feng's flak jacket, pulling the helmet down firmly over her head.

'Surround them!' she screamed. 'I want them alive.'

Most of the charging men did not even hear her. Some few did. A whistle shrilled. The charge wavered.

Leather-Vest emerged, pointing this way and that, directing an encircling movement. Selevan's sword flashed dangerously. If only the soldier's guns had fired, they could have felled him instantly. Now the silence of their rifles, the gloom of the dying sun, were intensifying their fear. They tightened their grip on their bayonets. The beginnings of panic flickered in their eyes. It would not be easy to control them, once Selevan shed a single drop of their blood.

Honesty was on her feet. 'They'll kill him, whatever she says. I know they will.'

'Is that Selevan with the sword?'

'Yes. And I think... he may be the Prince.'

'May be? Don't you *know?* I thought when he came...'

'So did I. I didn't think much of Selevan when I first saw him. But once he looks at you with those eyes... when he smiles...'

'If he's the Prince, then he can't be beaten, can he? He'll set us free.'

'I don't know any more. It's all going wrong. So many people are dead. And any moment, those soldiers are going to realize it isn't their commander up on that pile of stones yelling orders. Only Berlewen.'

'What if she is one of their officers now? One of THEM.'

'She never would be! Shut up! Oh, what can I *do?*'

'Help Father.' Colan knelt again, cradling his father's unconscious face in his thin hands.

Honesty looked down, then back at the inexorably closing ring of soldiers. 'If only Gawen was here. He came to help the wounded. But if we don't help Selevan, we'll all be dead.'

'You can't fight THEM. You haven't got a weapon.'

'I lost my spear. But there are plenty of stones.'

Keeping her head low, she crawled swiftly down through the shaking grass. At the foot of the hill she hesitated, casting round for something to throw. It was a pathetic gesture, but what else could she do?

The first rock had a more dramatic effect than she bargained for. She had aimed at a soldier's helmet. It struck him instead on the shoulder blade. He staggered, then spun round. The snarl when he saw her made other men turn.

Half a dozen broke off from the rest. They seemed glad of an excuse to leave the capture of Selevan with his flashing sword to others. They advanced towards her, menacingly slowly. They were big, tough, well-trained. Their bayonets swung level. They charged.

Honesty hurled the rest of her stones desperately. Then she was off, dodging, twisting, trying to stay on her feet and out of reach. She ran for her life.

She saw her mistake too late. The perimeter wall of the factory loomed up in her path. The soldiers were closing in on her. She saw the triumph in their eyes, under the shadow of their helmets. There was nowhere left to run.

Her eyes darted desperately left and right. Was that some alteration in the twilight along the wall? The factory gate! She lunged towards the opening. The gap between it and her seemed impossibly long. There were yells of victory from the men, certain she would never make it. A backward glance saw only the points of bayonets coming for her. A line of faces like angry bulls. She sprinted as she never had before.

She hurdled the fallen bodies more nimbly than the soldiers, burdened by their body armour. She was at the gate now, darting inside, frantically looking for a hiding place. The ominous stillness of the factory rose in front of her. No pounding pulse of machinery, no rolling smoke now. A monument to destruction. Where the weapons of death had piled off the assembly line, Honesty flung herself, seeking life.

Some heat from the extinguished furnaces lingered. The walls were black with smoke, the benches oily where Father and Colan had slaved.

She skidded on a patch of grease and fell, rather than dived, under a workbench. She crouched, panting. This was not what she meant to do. She did not want to be caught like an animal in its lair, trapped, helpless.

Too late now. With a roar, the men were in the doorway, blocking the scant daylight. They fanned out, with slow deliberation. They lowered their rifles, bayonets probing the shadows. She had only seconds left.

Tears blinded Colan as he watched her go, but he no longer had the strength to stop her. He bent over the inert body of his father. He had to bend his head very close to hear the whisper of breath.

'Father,' he murmured. 'What did they do to you?'

His hands moved the rags of clothing aside. He found the scars of beatings, which all the slaves bore. There was also an angry bruising on the back of his ribs, as though feet had trampled Luke in panic flight. That might mean snapped bones, injuries inside. There was a bruise on his head too, where he had fallen. Had this caused the coma into which he seemed to have slipped? Or was it just a deep fatal weariness?

Colan's head lifted high enough to look around for help. He found himself longing for a sight of the frail boy who had worked alongside him. Gonesek, too blind to fight. Gonesek, who had healing hands.

Berlewen grinned. The helmet was jammed down over her hair. The bullet-proof flak jacket shut out the unnaturally cold wind. For a mad moment she felt invincible. Leather-Vest was directing the soldiers to do what she ordered. She had saved the Prince's life, for precious moments at least.

They were dragging the prisoners towards her. She marvelled that Selevan managed to look noble, even in defeat. His hands were tied in front of him, his sword and helmet stripped from him, there was blood from a wound on his high forehead. His eyes were lowered. He held himself proudly unresisting as they shoved him in front of her.

Her heart ached for him. There must be something she could do to save her Prince, to save all of them, from the darkness in the hearts around her, as well as the darkness in the sky. But what? Then she caught sight of Leather-Vest, protectively close to Selevan. His head turned to her. The dark glasses hid his eyes but she read dismay in his face. She saw the quick flick of his wrist, motioning her away.

Berlewen suddenly realized the folly of her position. At the same moment, the advancing soldiers got the first clear sight of her face.

A single cry.

'It's the witch!'

The men instantly checked. They were still afraid of her, convinced she had conjured up the Ancoth. Then anger catapulted them forward. Leather-Vest came sprinting with them, the only friendly face in a sea of hate.

Every nerve in Berlewen screamed at her to jump down on the other side of the rubble and flee. But she was Berlewen St Kew Trethevy, Countess of Tintagel, and this was her moment of greatness. She would not run.

If a witch scared them, well then, she had better show them what she could do. And it would have to be quick. She flung her fingers out, pointing at the leading men.

'I summon the power of fire to silence your guns!'

Upwards. 'I summon the power of air to darken the sky!'

Out to the launches in the harbour. 'I summon the power of water to overwhelm you!'

Down. 'I summon the power of earth to open and swallow you all… unless you surrender your weapons. *Now!*'

The crack troops of THEM had been disciplined for years to obey commands without question. The authority in this girl's voice halted them. It was true. Their power was dissolving. The darkening midday sky terrified them. They felt again the marsh heaving under their feet, saw in vivid memory the Ancoth rising. It was all too strange, too horrible, too inexplicable. Had she done this?

The bayoneted rifles began to fall from unnerved hands.

Then Jude, the big lorry-driver, caught sight of the unconscious Feng. She had tumbled below the hillock, her helmet and jacket stripped away.

'Treachery! That's no witch. The girl's a terrorist!'

'We know what to do with traitors!'

'Kill the sun? We'll put out *her* light!'

For all their bravado, they were still scared. They closed in slowly. But they were coming for her.

'There she is! Under the bench!'

'Got you!'

Terrified, Honesty looked out and saw, not legs, but faces, lowered, peering, grinning. Big hands were reaching in to grab her and haul her out. She squirmed away. No use. They were on the other side of the workbench too. She was trapped.

'All right. I'm coming.'

At least, let me come out with dignity, avoid these grasping hands. Better not to think what happens next.

She started to crawl out from under the bench, but she was not quick enough. The soldiers lunged forward, grabbed her with meaty fists. Now they were hoisting her up on to the platform, where the overseers had stood. They were all six laughing obscenely, toying with their bayonets, enjoying her terror.

'Strap her up.'

'Let's take this nice and slow.'

'Make her squeal like a stuck pig.'

Two lashed her to a metal pillar that held up the roof. They had found whipcords, which cut her wrists viciously. It was useless to struggle. They only enjoyed it more.

The six jumped down and began to circle the dais slowly. They were looking up at her, laughing.

'Who's going first?'

'Toss for it.'

Let it be quick, Honesty prayed. Let me not weep or scream too much. Please!

She willed herself to concentrate on the doorway, to look up at the sky and not down at her tormentors. It was growing darker than ever, as if the sun itself was in mourning. Freedom is dying, she thought. This was our only chance.

Defiantly, she pursed her lips and tried to whistle the Prince's song. No sound would come from her trembling mouth. She tried to sing, but her throat was too dry.

There were roars of exultation and disappointment as the lot fell to the burliest of the men. He would strike the first blow. He was climbing on to the platform.

At last Honesty managed the ghost of a sound. Only a hum, and so shaky it was nearly impossible to recognize the tune. 'La la la-la, la-la-la la la.'

At least, the words could sing in her head. *One new morning our Prince will appear.*

And her Prince came.

Chapter Twenty-Nine

A storm of love burst through the open doorway. Slamming into the soldier who was advancing upon Honesty. Knocking him flying off the platform. Tail whirling, talons flailing, eyes blazing like yellow torches in the gloom.

The other five men charged towards the enkenethal, bayonets levelled. Prince whirled and leaped from the steps, sending them sprawling with his great paws. Now blood flew through the dim air from slashes in his bristling coat. His tail was a whipcord, his teeth daggers.

Honesty watched, delirious with joy and pride, as he herded the soldiers into a corner of the munitions shed and stood snarling over them.

Someone else ran in through the open doorway. He looked round swiftly. A boy not much older than Honesty. His one eye searched the gloom.

'Gawen!' she cried.

The young cowherd looked up then and grinned. 'What are you doing up there? They're all waiting for you outside.'

Through the blood thundering in her ears, Honesty could hear that the yells from the battlefield had taken on a new quality. They were still shouts of triumph, but not in the masculine bellow of the soldiers of THEM. Fresh voices sang through a range of pitches, men, women, even some high enough to be children. There was the whinny of horses. One familiar voice boomed like a foghorn above all the rest.

'What's a gel of mine doing in that ridiculous uniform? Take it off at once, Berlewen!'

'The *duchess?*'

Gawen laughed. He grabbed up a fallen rifle, unhooked its bayonet and vaulted on to the platform. 'Here. Allow me.'

He cut her free. His warm hands smelt now both of the cowshed and of astringent ointment. Dazed with shock, dazzled with light, though the sun was hardly visible, she let him steady her down the steps and lead her out into the open. An amazing sight met her.

Berlewen told herself afterwards that she had not intended to run away. She had only recoiled instinctively as the helmeted soldiers charged towards her. A stone in the rubble had given way, starting a slide down the pile which had carried her with it, tumbling fast, out of control.

She lay on her back, helpless, with the rush of stones bouncing down around her. All she could see was the dull sky above her, light draining away like water in sand. Her life was leaching with it. All their lives.

The mound of rubble hid everything else from her. Why was there no line of furious faces breaking over the top of it? Where had the soldiers gone?

The sound seemed to come to her out of that

vault of the sky. A trumpet call.

A host of angels? she wondered dazedly.

'A Trethevy! A Trethevy!'

Berlewen sat up.

'Cornwall!'

'Kernow for ever!'

She scrambled back up the hillock as fast as she could go.

It was as though the tide had come in over a grey mudflat. Even without the sun, the colours sparkled. A host of horsemen and women, on little moorland ponies. And a whole infantry of peasants with pitchforks, fishermen with boathooks, housemaids with broomsticks, grooms with whips. There were footmen with gilt buttons on their livery, stable boys with hay in their hair. Honesty's grandfather, in his red and black trousers, was wielding a scythe like old Father Time.

A handful of soldiers firing guns could have massacred them in moments. But the rifles were useless now, except as stocks for bayonets. At close quarters, the guns were too short to reach the wielders of long-handled weaponry snatched up from barns and kitchens. The people of Tintagel swarmed over the battlefield, like stinging ants smothering the bodies of larger insects.

In the centre of it all, directing operations from a fat pony, sat the improbable figure of Berlewen's father. Gone was his elegant hunter, destroyed by THEM. But the duke had dressed himself splendidly to rescue his daughter, with ruffles of lace at his throat and a silver breastplate which had hung from the panelling in the Great Hall as long as Berlewen could remember. He was brandishing an ancient sword, also from the hall. It had never occurred to Berlewen that anyone would draw it in anger. Indeed, the duke himself looked rather uncomfortable with it, as though he was not quite sure what he was supposed to do with it.

The duchess, on the other hand, looked magnificently in her element. A cavalier's helmet was clamped on her silver wig, from which nodded three ostrich plumes. One of them had broken and was falling over her eye. The shield she flourished sported a rampant boar. Her mount was, of necessity, bigger than her husband's, though being still a pony, he hung his head wearily under the weight of his formidable rider and her armour. Armed with a three-pronged fishing spear, she was an impressive reincarnation of Britannia.

Berlewen gaped.

She was just wondering what she could do to help, where she should throw herself into the fray, when someone spotted her. It was Honesty's grandfather, waving his scythe in alarming circles round his head.

'Up there! On that hillock! She'll be one of THEIR leaders!'

The peasant army swarmed like bees. They were all round the pile of rubble where she stood. Pronged weapons were reaching up, stabbing. Their faces were full of fury.

'BERLEWEN!' She heard her mother yell, louder than the dinner gong that had reverberated throughout the castle.

Tintagel's people quailed instantly at that voice. Heads turned away from Berlewen. Weapons faltered.

The duchess advanced upon her daughter, her

withering scorn taking in the uniform of THEM, grey trousers in an unnatural fabric, the white shirt, though now decidedly grubby, the beetle-browed helmet, the bullet-proof jacket.

'All right! All right!' Berlewen shouted, blushing and scowling. She tore off the flak jacket, tugged the grey helmet from her cropped head. 'It wasn't my idea. THEY took my clothes away and made me wear this disgusting uniform. And then I had to dress up as Feng to stop them killing the Prince.' She looked round in alarm. 'What's happened to him? Where's Selevan?'

The crowd parted. Selevan, his hands cut free, mounted now on a white pony, was led forward. Cheers broke out, from Tom and the remnant from Glastonbury, then from the massed Cornish troop. Lastly the slaves punched their fists in the air and took up the ragged shout. Selevan raised his hand and shook his head.

Blood had poured down his face, drying stiffly when the wound had been staunched. He was pale but grim, his head held high. The words came with difficulty.

'Madam,' he bowed to Berlewen. 'I must thank you for my life... and your noble parents.'

From beside Selevan's pony, Leather-Vest grinned up at him. His own arms were bound now. They had taken him prisoner. He, like Berlewen, wore the hated uniform of THEM. There was blood on his leather-clad chest, bruises on his face. One lens of the dark glasses was smashed.

'We're all one family. We helped each other.'

The Cornish crowd showed bewilderment.

'Is he the Prince's friend?' asked Honesty's grandfather. 'Him?'

'Let him go!' Berlewen ordered. 'He's the truest friend I ever had... Except for Petal,' her heart murmured.

Selevan hung his head over the pony's mane now, as the weariness of disappointment overcame him. 'I have failed. I lost hundreds of good people, crossing the marsh. In the end, it wasn't I who freed the factory but the slaves themselves.'

'You sang the Prince's song, even when it looked hopeless,' called a small clear voice from the edge of the crowd. Honesty lifted her head bravely. 'They heard you. You gave them hope.'

'But the Prince didn't come,' said Selevan bitterly.

There was a shock of surprise. Doubt rippled across the sea of faces. Heads turned to question each other and then stared back at him.

It was Honesty's grandfather who spoke for them all, planting the handle of his scythe on the ground and leaning over it. 'Begging your pardon, sir, but bain't you the Prince? The one we've waited for all these years?'

An expression of consternation crossed Selevan's sensitive face. 'Me? Whatever made you think that? I've never claimed to be. I've given my life to serving him, shed my blood for him. But I've never seen him, any more than you have. I just believed with all my heart that if we rose against THEM, he'd have to come.'

Berlewen felt her heart sink with disbelief. Uncertainty was spreading to all of them now. They had all been so sure, the labourers in the Cornish fields, the slaves in the factory, the rebels training for warfare on Glastonbury. They had all found the courage to sing the Prince's song, they had risked their lives for him. They had staked everything on the certain hope that he would appear when they needed him.

'What if there isn't a Prince?' called a voice from the crowd.

'Maybe that's why the sun is dying.'

'Suppose the Prince is dead too!'

A long groan shuddered from hundreds of throats as they turned their faces to the sky.

Honesty looked round in desperation. It was getting hard to see. Gawen had disappeared from her side. Where was her father? And Colan? She had left them somewhere over there, in the long grass at the foot of the hill. Had the killing reached them? Was her father still alive?

She could dimly make out activity still going on at that far side of the battlefield. The fighting was finished in the no-man's-land outside the factory. The soldiers had been disarmed and tied up. They sat now, buzzing like angry wasps, against the factory wall. The mood of the victorious troops had sobered. The ground was strewn with dead, of both sides. There were a daunting number of wounded needing attention. Gawen the cowherd would be back there with them.

Honesty could not see properly through the unnatural dusk, but she made out a stooping figure, giving what help he could. She went towards him. She was quite close before she could distinguish that the figure was indeed familiar, but not the boy she expected.

'Colan!' She ran to her brother. Even before she reached him, an urgent question was jolted from her. 'Where's Father? Why have you left him?'

Colan turned. His long steady look, unsmiling, told her what she did not want to know. She went into her brother's arms and they held each other.

'I don't think he felt anything. He wasn't mortally wounded. He just didn't have any strength left, once he'd seen us outside the gates. If only Gonesek had been here. He has healing hands.'

'Gonesek?'

'The half-blind slave who workcd next to me. But you feel that even with one dodgy eye he can see more than the rest of the world does with two good eyes.'

'I've met him, with the burial party. He took my message.'

Honesty looked into her brother's eyes and then pulled herself gently away from him. She walked over to the foot of the hill and followed Colan's beaten track through the grass until she found her father.

'At least he saw freedom, even if it was only for a few minutes.'

'Father was always free, no matter what THEY did to him.'

She bent to kiss his still face. 'Go well,' she whispered, 'into peace.'

She stood up and shook the tears from her eyes. Colan was standing behind her.

'Let's get on with the living,' she said. 'There are an awful lot of wounded.'

Among the bodies a figure was kneeling with his back to them, beside a fallen man.

'There's Gawen,' Honesty asserted confidently, hurrying forward.

'Gawen?'

'A cowherd from Glastonbury, with an eye-patch and a knapsack full of bandages and ointments. He risked his life to rescue me and Berlewen, the night the Dragon-From-Under nearly got us.'

'No. It's...'

The boy turned as they approached and raised his bloodied hand in greeting. Honesty stopped in surprise. He was skeletally lean, his clothes ragged. There was no black eye-patch, revealing Gawen's sparkling grin in his good brown eye. Instead, a milky blindness, with Gonesek's wisdom smiling up from his unfocussed green one.

'I could use some help.' The smile, they saw now, was weary. 'So many wounds. You'd think, to read the storybooks, that there was something romantic about swords and spears, but not when you see what they do to real people. To say nothing of bayonets and pitchforks.'

In silence, Colan and Honesty knelt beside him, and steeled themselves to do what they could to help.

'I don't want to worry you both,' Colan broke in after a while. 'But I can hardly see what I'm doing. Isn't it ever going to get light again? It was always horrible in the factory, but I thought, once we'd got outside...'

All three looked up at the sky over the factory. It was as dark as the slate roof. It would have been less threatening if there had been heavy cloud. But there was not. The sun was a pale ghost of a disc that hardly penetrated the gloom. It gave no warmth, and its light was dwindling, fainter and fainter.

'What's happening to the sun?' whispered Honesty. 'I thought... I know it sounds silly... I thought once we'd won, and the slaves were free, it would all be wonderful, like never before. The sun would blaze out and the whole world would be golden and laughing, and everybody would dance for joy.'

'Did you?' said Gonesek drily. 'Is that what you think war is?' He peered along the lines of wounded, still crying for attention, at the resentful knots of prisoners, at the slumped figures of the slaves, too exhausted to share in the rejoicing. 'We can try to heal some of these wounds, but the scars will be terrible.'

'It was the Ancoth.' Berlewen startled them, standing over them. 'The Dragon-From-Under,' she added for Colan's benefit. 'That's when it started. I think She's swallowed all the fire in the world. She rose up, when we were all crossing the marsh. She didn't do anything, just opened Her mouth wide and… looked at us. When She sank out of sight, THEIR guns wouldn't fire. Nothing has ever been the same since. That's when the sun started to die.'

'That's horrible,' Honesty shivered.

Gonesek raised his eyebrows. It was hard to tell which one he was looking at. 'You wouldn't be alive without Her, would you? Not you, Honesty, not Colan, not Berlewen. If She hadn't swallowed THEIR fire of death…'

'But does She have to swallow the sun too?'

'Creation is all of piece. You can't just pick and choose the laws that suit you.'

'But the sun will come back again, won't it?' Colan asked urgently. 'We can't live like this. If it gets colder and colder, nothing will grow. Even the furnaces in the factory went out. We won't be able to light a fire to warm ourselves. We'll die.'

'There must be something we can do!' stormed Berlewen.

Gonesek's clever fingers went on bandaging the shattered leg of a soldier of THEM. He smiled softly and said nothing.

Chapter Thirty

The duchess's ringing voice made them turn. 'And what, precisely, shall we do about *that?*' She pointed dramatically at the small bound figure at her feet.

'Feng!' cried Berlewen. 'I'd forgotten about her.'

She ran to the crowd gathered round the hillock of rubble, with the duke and duchess standing magnificently on its summit. Honesty and Colan, more weary, followed her slowly.

Feng had recovered consciousness after the blow from Berlewen's handcuffs. Her arms and legs had been bound, her mouth gagged. She sat on the stony ground, her dark eyes flashing anger at the faces looming above her.

'Look at her!' the duchess invited her followers. 'That's THEM, for you. A top leader of the Supreme Council for Justice and Peace. That's what you were afraid of.'

'No, it wasn't,' muttered Honesty's grandfather. 'It was they guns.'

'What shall we do with her, my dear?' asked the duke.

All around them, the crowd bayed.

'Kill her, of course!'

'String her up from a lamp post.'

'Roast her over a slow fire.'

'There bain't no fire, you fool,' Grandfather reminded his neighbour.

'Gut her like a mackerel, then!'

Berlewen stood over the prisoner, who had been her captor. She looked pale and anxious. 'I know how you all feel. That's what THEY did to us.'

'What are we waiting for, then?'

Berlewen lifted her head and looked out over their upturned faces. She could no longer see any horizon on the blackening sea. Night was advancing, so dark that it might be the death of daylight.

'But…' said Honesty's clear voice out of the shadows, 'do we want to be like THEM?'

'What do you suggest?' shouted a freed slave. 'Let them go, to do it all again? Thousands died inside that factory, murdered by THEM.'

'Honesty's right. If we're like THEM too…' Berlewen plucked at those uniform garments she still wore, the grey trousers, the white shirt, the tie, as though they were the coils of a snake tightening around her.

'If your enkenethal hadn't come charging along, we'd all be dead by now. You outside the factory, as well as us inside. THEY've got no pity, THEM.'

'Petal?' cried Berlewen. 'He's *here?* Where?'

Honesty clapped her hands to her mouth. 'In the factory! I forgot all about him. Oh, Prince, how could I? He came hurtling in through the door, just as the first soldier was climbing up to get me. He was wonderful, like a real Prince. And then he penned them all in a corner, like a flock of sheep. He's still guarding them.'

Leather-Vest, newly freed, sprang in the direction of the gate. 'Leave it to me.'

'But I left him on Glastonbury. And what are you doing here from Cornwall?' Berlewen rounded on her mother and father. 'How did you know about the uprising and that we desperately needed help?' But a conviction was starting to grow joyously in her heart.

'Would you believe it was your enkenethal, my dear?' The duke beamed. 'He came bounding into the stable yard where I was overseeing things.'

'Lambasting us for not mucking out the straw smartly enough for his High-and-Mightiness,' muttered Honesty's grandfather.

'You know THEY killed all the horses, the day you left? Terrible business. Barbarians! We had to smuggle some ponies down off the moor after they'd gone.'

'Have you seen that poor beast he's riding?' Grandfather chuckled. 'Likely to buckle at the knees, under all that fat.'

'Shh!' said Honesty.

'Anyway, my dear, that enkenethal of yours comes bounding into the yard and flings himself on me, barking like a fiend. Then he's rounding everybody up and starts tugging me by the trousers towards the gate.'

'Clever boy!'

'It was your mother who twigged on. She came marching out of the castle and saw at once what was needed. Splendid woman. "Get yourselves weapons," she cries. "Whatever you can find that'll do damage. Saddle those nags. Pack plenty of food." Didn't ask where we were going or what for. Just knew the Trethevys were needed. So we rode out of the castle, with the banner of Cornwall flying, ready for anything.'

'Didn't Prince tell you why?' Honesty asked.

Grandfather nudged her. 'They don't think an enkenethal can speak, do they? So they never listen.'

Moments later, a little procession came stumbling out into the open. Six over-large soldiers, whose uniforms now seemed to droop from their defeated bodies. Hands over their heads. Leather-Vest strolled alongside, like a nonchalant shepherd boy. Behind them padded the magnificent enkenethal. The scarlet ridge on his back was erect, his tail held in a stiff upward curve. His purple-rimmed nostrils flared. He was growling softly and the soldiers shuddered and stumbled at the sound.

At the sight of him, the crowd drew back. Their faces had been alight with welcome, but were now half scared.

The enkenethal paced slowly past his own prisoners and reached the foot of the pile where Feng squatted helplessly among the fallen bricks. She shrank back from his approach. He stood towering over her, his monstrous muzzle hanging above her head.

'What shall I do, Petal?' pleaded Berlewen. 'I don't want to be like THEM. And I nearly was. The Ancoth would have swallowed me, if it hadn't been for you.'

'So?' said the enkenethal in a deep growl.

'Because you loved me, She let me go. I'd have to let Feng live, if you loved her.'

The little commander looked up with proud defiance.

'Do *you* love her, Berlewen?'

'… No!'

The gloom was so deep, she could see little but his

236

great golden eyes. Petal bent and licked Feng's pale gagged face.

'*Do* you love her, Berlewen?'

'N-no. At least, not if love means having a nice feeling about her, I don't.'

'Do you *love* her, Berlewen?'

She stared into his eyes. Slowly she began to walk down the mound of rubble to Feng's side. She bent in silence and unbound the gag that was biting into the woman's gums.

'If love is what I think you mean, an act of will, yes.'

The faintest beam of sunlight crept over the ground, making soft shadows alongside the scattered stones. Hundreds of faces turned to it, hungry for the touch of warmth, the beginning of hope.

'The sun!'

'It's coming back!'

'It's not going to die!'

There were whoops of joy, weapons tossed into the air. People were hugging each other.

But Colan cried, 'Wait a minute! You haven't understood what it means. If the sun comes back, fire will too. Everything's going to be like it was before. The guns, all THEIR machines, the furnaces. We'll be THEIR slaves again.'

Fear swept over the crowd, like a storm bowing a field of hay.

'He's right.'

'Better to put up with the dark.'

'Kill them all, I say.'

The sunbeam darkened. A chill wind blew off the sea. Berlewen looked down at Feng. She held out her hand and pulled the bound officer to her feet. Her fingers busied themselves with the knots, untied Feng's hand and feet. The crowd was grumbling restlessly, closing in.

The teenage girl was taller than the grown woman. Berlewen bent her head and spoke to Feng steadily.

'You're not the only one who wanted power over people. It's not just THEM. It's us. Me. I never thought about it until I knew Honesty. I go hot and cold when I think how I used to treat servants. If I can't forgive you, I'd be saying that I couldn't ever be forgiven myself.'

She held out her arms awkwardly and hugged Feng.

The shaft of sunlight strengthened, crept up the factory walls.

'What about us?' yelled one of the slaves, pulling up the rags of his shirt. 'Don't you care? Look at these scars! Look around you at all the dead! It's not just up to you.'

'We want to be free!' voices yelled.

Honesty was suddenly beside Berlewen on the mound, holding Colan by the hand. 'Luke Olds was my father. You all knew him in the factory. He died today. But listen to what Colan says about him.' She turned, challenging her brother.

Colan spread out his hands helplessly. 'It's true. You saw him. You know Luke Olds was always free. In his heart.'

Berlewen was still gazing at Feng, willing herself to act out a love her heart still could not feel. 'What will you do if we set you free?'

Feng licked her lips, bruised from the gag. She blinked away the tears in her eyes proudly.

'You are right. I have known power. The authority of

a member of the Supreme Council, interrogating prisoners, riding through streets in an armoured vehicle, seeing people cower away from me in fear. When I saw the Ancoth swallow the strength of the sun and the force of fire, I thought that was a more terrible power. Now, I see the sun begin to shine again, because of one single act of love. I know where the greatest power lies.'

The enkenethal pushed against the back of her legs. His tail whirled in joyful circles. The sunshine was spreading, beginning to catch the edge of the ripples in the harbour basin.

'I am only one officer,' Feng warned. 'No one else on the Council has seen what I have. There's no reason to believe you will change THEIR hearts. I can only promise you my own help. It may not last, but I will do what I can. From this moment, I declare the West is free.'

Cheers roared to the sky.

Then arguments broke out. 'What about all these soldiers?'

'And Headquarters. As soon as THEIR guns can fire again…'

'We'll be risking everything.'

Berlewen turned her face up to feel the sunshine. 'Yes! But look where risk has got us, so far.'

'Spoken like a Trethevy!' cheered her mother.

'It won't last.'

'It never does.' The mutters of resentment could be heard from every side.

Berlewen lowered her stare to the rebellious crowd. 'No. There will be times of night. I know. I've been a slave in Headquarters. But even at the darkest, we have to believe that the morning will come. We can help it happen. Now, just in this place, and at this moment, the sun is shining.'

She lifted her head and the shaft of light fell on her. Bareheaded, dusty, younger than almost all the faces turned up to her, she nevertheless looked commanding.

A strong voice rang from the crowd. It was Tom, Selevan's second-in-command. 'Don't you see? It wasn't a Prince we were waiting for all this time. It was a Princess!'

There was a moment of astonishment. Then cheers thundered against the factory walls, rolled out across the water, echoed back from the hills.

'A Princess!'

'Our Princess has come!'

'This is the day!'

Berlewen's face was horrified. She struggled to speak above the noise. 'No! You've got it wrong! I'm not the Prince. I was horrible to people. Ask Honesty. The real Prince would never have been like that. Never!'

Tom's shout cut through the rest. 'So you're saying the song was all a lie? There never was a Prince?'

'I think there is.'

The enkenethal padded down off the mound of rubble. The crowd retreated before him, like the tide dropping down a beach. His purple ears lifted proudly in the weak sunshine, showing the scars of THEIR bullets. Light danced along the ruby red ridge of his back. His tail swung eagerly. His two gigantic front paws kept lifting, one after the other, as though he had to restrain himself from breaking into a gallop.

Honesty stared down into his brilliant eyes.

'Where, Prince? Who is he? The real Prince?'

'I think you know.'

'What's that?' The duke seemed to start into life, as though from a trance. 'Did that animal say something?'

'I think,' said Honesty carefully, 'he's trying to tell us the Prince is here among us. Now.'

The enkenethal's gums parted, his tongue panted. He might have been grinning.

'Who?'

People were turning to each other, puzzled, questioning.

'The duke?'

'The duchess, more like. She's got guts, that one.'

'Don't be daft!'

'I was certain sure it was Selevan, but he won't have it.'

Honesty's clear young voice was carried over their heads on the breeze. 'Just for a while, when I got caught up in the fighting, I thought it might be Selevan too. I wanted a hero with a sword and a helmet, to make me feel safe and brave. Only now I remember that when I first saw him, I didn't feel like that. Why couldn't I see it? There was somebody else I felt from the beginning I could trust with my life.'

'Who?'

'Prince knows.'

Chapter Thirty-One

As if he had only been waiting for this, the enkenethal barked. His tail began to swing dangerously. Huge taloned paws scored the ground as he began to turn. The crowd parted swiftly, opening a path, through which he trotted. The awkward legs were gathering themselves to launch into a canter. Dust flew in all directions as he careered across the rubble-strewn ground towards the factory.

'Petal!'

'Where's he going?'

Free of the crowd, the enkenethal's leaps were getting longer and longer, ragged ears streaming back. He was galloping straight for the gate.

'What's he doing?' called Colan. 'There's no one left inside.'

Berlewen was running after him, with Honesty and Colan just behind her. The curious crowd flocked with them, jostling the duke and duchess, who were trying to keep up.

Colan shuddered as the shadow of the huge solid gates towered over him. The returning sunshine of late afternoon had fallen gently on him, but here a cold persisted that struck into his bones. The other slaves hesitated too, unwilling even now to trust themselves again inside that place of horror. The servants and peasants of Tintagel were bolder, but even they slowed. As they looked up to the receding sky, they felt themselves dwarfed by the height of those walls.

Petal did not hesitate, bounding over the oily muck of the cobbled yard. As the factory buildings closed around them, those at the front of the crowd became aware of a new sensation. The fragrant smell of cooking was drifting along the dark alleyways.

'Never mind searching for the Prince. Looks like he's after a square meal,' chuckled Grandfather.

Steam was creeping from a lower building at the far end of the passageway. Colan knew it to be the kitchen. Out of it had come greasy vats of thin soup, watery, disgusting, with little more nourishment than the stalks of cabbages. Alongside this was cooked the rich meaty meals which put such gleaming flesh on the faces of the security guards and overseers.

Now the fires were alight again in the kitchen ranges and that same maddeningly delicious smell was filling the air. The savoury steam of beef and onions, the mouth-watering fragrance of new-baked bread, the sweet smell of apples and spices stewing.

The crowd slowed, breathing in great gulps of it.

'Never knew I was so hungry.' Grandfather's stomach rumbled. 'We've marched a mighty long way on bread and cheese.'

Colan's eyes watered. 'Who's in there? Is somebody still cooking food for THEM?'

There was a growl of anger, running back through the crowd.

'Prince is going to find out,' Honesty told them.

Several leaps from the kitchen door, the enkenethal had slowed. Still he went forward, whining softly, as though he longed to break in through the door and yet was afraid. The big paws lifted more reluctantly. His yellow belly sank nearer the ground.

'What are you afraid of, Petal?' said Berlewen. 'Who's inside?'

'Thought he was taking us to this Prince you're all talking about,' grumbled Duke Gwalather.

Petal's questing nose had reached the door. It was almost closed, but unlatched. The smell of cooking was wafting out through the gap, almost unbearably rich now, as if you might eat the smell itself.

The door trembled. Petal pushed harder. As it swung suddenly wide open, steam hung a curtain before them. Warm, inviting, it sprang out into the cold air of the shadowed passage. Up it spiralled, spreading, dissipating, scattering its bounty into the freshly blue sky.

The air in the kitchen was clearing.

Petal was down on the floor now, still creeping forward, whining faster as though fearful, and yet his tasselled tail thumping the ground with joy.

A slight figure stood in front of the enormous cooking stove, his back to them as he stirred the pots. The coarse apron, in which he had wrapped himself, seemed too large for him. It was hard to be sure what he was wearing underneath. He moved deftly from one saucepan to another, opened the oven door swiftly, releasing another waft of apples and spices and baking bread, and closed it again. Sunlight was struggling through the clouded windows. It fell on the huge kitchen table and lit the jugs of golden cider.

Petal wriggled closer, as though he could hardly restrain himself from flinging his weight on the boy, and yet could not quite summon up the courage.

Berlewen, Honesty and Colan stopped in the doorway. The crowd was pushing behind them, struggling to see.

'Is he in there?'

'That's never our Prince, is it? In an apron?'

Berlewen was gazing longingly past the enkenethal. There was something familiar about that slender back, those busy hands.

'Leather-Vest?' she said wonderingly.

'Gawen?' 'Gonesek?' Honesty and Colan breathed simultaneously.

Petal was almost at the kitchen boy's heels. As he turned, waving his wooden spoon in greeting, the enkenethal leaped. The slight figure was lost under a storm of grey fur, panting pink tongue and wildly circling tail which threatened to sweep the jugs from the table.

'I love you too!' laughed a voice from behind the maelstrom.

The boy had his arms round Petal's neck. The enkenethal's gigantic straining body still blotted out most of the rest as he frantically licked the boy's face. The crowd was utterly still. Over the frenzied animal's shoulder the upper part of a head began to appear. Two eyes danced with laughter.

There was an astonished silence.

'If Leather-Vest took off his sunglasses...'

'If Gawen didn't have an eyepatch...'

'If both Gonesek's eyes were clear...'

Like the sun returning to the world out of the noonday darkness, the two eyes smiled at them, one green, one brown.

'Map!' cried Colan and Honesty together.

The tide of the enkenethal's enthusiasm was falling at last. The boy laid his hand on Petal's head and caressed his ears.

'Seen you somewhere before, haven't I?' The Duke of Cornwall scratched his head where the helmet had left a purple circle.

'Nonsense,' said the duchess. 'I never forget a face. I can assure you, if I had ever met our Prince, I'd certainly know him.'

'You're the *bootboy*!' said Berlewen, staring at Map.

'Then you were... Gonesek?' said Colan. 'You were always with us. Even though you seemed to be the weakest of us all. In the sweat of the factory. In the barracks after we were flogged. You were flogged yourself! But when you massaged my shoulders, I felt... healed.'

'I called you a coward,' Honesty blushed. 'When Gawen... when you... wouldn't fight. And yet you were in the front line, rescuing those who had fallen, under the noses of the enemy. I always did feel safe with you, from the beginning, in the boat at Glastonbury. But I didn't think.... Well, you were just the cowherd, not much different from me.'

'No, Honesty,' said Map quietly. 'You are not much different from me.'

Berlewen blushed hotly. 'The first time I noticed you was the day I threw my boots at Honesty. I hit her. I didn't care about the bruises and the mud. I was only thinking about myself and how unhappy I was. You cleaned my boots and gave them back to me, polished and shining. And you taught me to sing the Prince's song.'

'But Honesty taught you the first line, and Honesty's grandfather the second,' he prompted her.

'The Prince?' The murmur was running through the mass of people pushing and standing on tiptoe to see him. 'Is *that* the Prince?'

'Map? From below stairs?' marvelled the laundress from Tintagel.

'Where's his crown then? Where's his magic sword?' demanded the rebels. 'How's he going to lead us to victory?'

'Is he the real Prince? Come to rule us justly, after all this time?' the freed slaves wondered.

'No!' shouted Berlewen, spinning round to face them and stamping her foot. 'Haven't you been listening? He hasn't just *come* to rule us. He was with us all the time. I met him even in the Headquarters of THEM. I thought I was utterly alone, without a single friend. But he was there.'

People were pushing forward now. Tom and some of the rebels broke through into the kitchen and tried to hoist Map on to their shoulders. He stepped lightly aside, dancing out of their reach.

'Excuse me. I've got the dinner to cook. You must all be starving.'

'Let me help,' said Honesty, rolling up her sleeves.

'That bread smells nearly ready.'

'Never mind that,' said the duke to Map. 'If you're really the Prince, we can't have you mucking about in the kitchen. Let the little people do that, skivvies and potboys and thingummies. You'd better call a council, get up on a throne and start ruling. It's about time somebody straightened out this country.'

Petal stood tall, his whole coat bristling with warning, blocking their way. Map stroked him fondly.

'I think it's about time you all had a square meal. Can't you see the slaves are dropping with hunger?' This time his eyes did not smile at them.

Colan tried to move a heavy saucepan, but there was no strength in his arms. Map moved to help him.

Berlewen put out a hand and grasped his sleeve.

'We need a leader. Somebody's got to take charge of these people. I know I'm not fit to take the crown and be their ruler. But you are.'

Map raised his eyebrows to a great height. One green eye, one brown, twinkled.

'I think you have missed the point, Countess,' he said gently. 'Being the Prince isn't what you thought it was. It's not about sitting on a throne. Not about giving orders and sending everybody running. Not leading a war. It's being *with* your people, all of them, wherever they are, sharing their suffering, bearing as much of it for them as you can. The ruler of all must be the servant of all.'

The fire, restored, leaped in the range behind him. The sun was travelling down the western sky. Glad golden light streamed across the damaged city, lit sparkles like diamonds in the granite walls that had shut in the slaves. It fell full through the doorway on to Map's face, making jewels of his eyes, emerald and topaz, the only jewels he would ever consent to wear.

'Then who *will* rule us?' Berlewen demanded. 'Somebody's got to give the orders, enforce the laws, direct the defences.'

'THEY'll give the orders, as soon as they get THEIR firepower back. That's one thing you can be sure of,' Tom growled.

Berlewen did not take her eyes off Map. 'Who?' she insisted.

'The best of leaders never try to do everything by themselves. People grow as you give them responsibility. I have shown you the laws by which this world was made to run. Now I need delegates to carry on my work. Some people will muck out stables in my name, read bedtime stories in my name, keep account books in my name, yes, and govern a country in my name.'

'Who?' Berlewen repeated.

He gazed at her steadily, no longer laughing. 'Let it be someone who knows what it is to suffer.'

The enkenethal stalked towards Colan and seized his thin arm. The scrawny, hollow-faced teenager started back. It needed only a little of the beast's strength to tug him reluctantly to the doorstep, where he stood, scared and embarrassed, facing the crowd.

'Someone who knows what it is to serve.'

'Me?' squeaked Honesty, as her four-footed Prince came for her. 'But I wouldn't know how. I'm just a chambermaid.'

'You made a pretty good job of getting me safely to Glastonbury,' Berlewen muttered, blushing again.

To the astonishment of everyone who knew her, she went down on one knee before the brother and sister.

'And someone who has learned what it means to love, by an effort of will.'

Petal's snout butted the young countess, none too gently, so that she almost tumbled forward over Honesty's feet. She scrambled round to protest indignantly, but Petal snapped his yellow teeth.

'On your feet... ma'am!'

The huge animal had all three of them now, shocked into silence. They stood on the raised step, like a trio of sheep separated out from the flock. Petal turned to grin at Map, his tongue quivering with satisfaction. Map patted him on the head.

'Oh, by the way,' he said, ducking under the kitchen table. 'I can't offer you golden sceptres, but will a pilgrim staff do instead?'

He straightened up, holding out three stout sticks. The two girls stared with astonished recognition, then reached out eagerly for theirs. Colan followed more wonderingly. The plain wood felt truer to the hand than gold.

'Hold fast to them, this time,' laughed Map.

Doubt was still running across the faces of the crowd. A Prince, found and lost again, in a few heartbeats. Three teenagers to rule them. The power of THEM coming back as the sun beat hotter and hotter on their faces.

Selevan was the first to move. The rebel commander went down on his knees in the greasy yard.

'As soon as I find what they did with my sword when they captured me, I'll offer it up to you. Command me as you will. In the name of the Prince, I pledge you my loyal service.'

The enkenethal's tail began to wag.

The duke looked at the duchess, who was wiping the dirt from his face with her lace-edged handkerchief. 'Well, my dear, there's a Trethevy among them, though I can't say I remember the like of her in our family before. At least one of them's got noble blood.'

'Gwalather,' boomed the duchess sternly, 'I think you've missed the point.'

With a magnificent flourish of her brocaded skirts she swept a curtsey to her chambermaid and Colan, then to her own daughter.

'Cornwall will be true to the death... *Gwalather!*'

'Oh... yes. Yes, of course.' The duke had more trouble bending his knee, but he managed to present to them the antique sword taken from the castle hall, though not without a little reluctance. Berlewen motioned Honesty to move forward. Scarlet with embarrassment, the chambermaid touched the offered hilt.

'Er... thank you.' She handed it back to the duke extremely quickly.

Tom and Livvy, the rebel captains, knelt in turn.

Then, surprising everyone, a small dark-clad figure pushed her way forward. Feng went down and laid her forehead to the ground at their feet.

Raising her dirtied face again, she said, 'I am sorry. I am truly sorry. And I have never said that word to anyone since I entered the service of THEM. I shall try to prove it. I offer to command as many of these soldiers as wish to join your cause. Or if you want me to go back to Headquarters and confront THEM in your name, I am ready to do that.'

Berlewen held out her hand, unable to speak. Then Petal bounded past the three and slammed his paws into Feng's shoulders, knocking her over. He licked the dust from her face, her hands, her feet, till she could not help rolling over on her side to defend herself, helpless with laughter.

Now Grandfather, even more stiffly than the duke, was beginning to kneel, trying not to endanger his neighbours with his scythe. Rank after rank, rebels, footmen, farm workers, slaves, and even, the three saw with astonishment, some of the captured soldiers, knelt in homage to their young rulers.

Honesty looked round in alarm for Map. He was where she should have known he would be, with his sleeves rolled up, hard at work in front of the kitchen stove.

'I've made a big pot of broth for the wounded. Can you help me? It'll put the heart back into them.'

Berlewen and Honesty each seized a handle. Colan picked up a ladle and as many bowls as he could carry.

'Lead on.'

They heaved the cauldron out of the sweetly smoking kitchen. As they crossed the yard its fragrance spread round them. The slaves watched it with huge hungry eyes. Tom and Livvy were already piling meat and potatoes on to plates on the table for them. The duchess was carving an apple pie.

As they came out of the gates to where the wounded were lying, the sun was sinking lower, bathing the sky in a glory of purple and gold. Soon it must set. Berlewen lifted her face defiantly. The brilliance lit her eyes.

'We will serve you,' she called to all of them in a clear strong voice. 'The three of us, as well as we can. While the light still shines in the West, and when the darkness falls, we will work for you. We were waiting for a Prince who would set us free, but he has shown us that we always were free. No one can take that away from us. Whatever happens to us, the Prince will always rule where it counts, in the country of our hearts, as long as we keep singing his song.'

As they gave the steaming broth to those who could not walk, from wounds or weakness, the sun blazed out from under the last clouds. It turned the sea to gold. And all across the bay the surface of the water began to dance. Little ripples ran and skittered, catching jewels of light in their fingers. The waves rose higher, seahorses now, with foaming white crests beginning to stream along their necks. Breakers were rearing, taller and taller, while everyone watched in astonishment.

'What's happening?' cried Grandfather. 'The sea's alive!'

Up through the walls of glass-green water a figure was rising that was greener still. A gigantic crested head. A neck that was long enough to peer over the island in the middle of the bay. Shoulders that flashed in the sunset, not only green now, but all the iridescent colours of an opal: purple and sky blue, rose and jade. The enormous eyes widened, golden and black and brilliant. The Ancoth was laughing at them.

There was not one sound from the shore. Awe and amazement held them all in its grip. They gazed and gazed. Then, with a flick of Her tail that swept up the craft in the harbour and sent them leaping, the Dragon-

From-Under dived again and plunged for the west. They saw the colossal wake of Her progress rolling surf far up the shores. Even the trees on the banks bowed as She passed.

Colan waved his ladle in farewell. 'It looks as if we've made Her happy at last.'

'Is She really going?' breathed Honesty. 'Does that mean Glastonbury's... safe?'

'Nothing's ever safe,' said Berlewen. 'We're going to need a lot of courage.'

Far out to sea, the breakers were parting for the Ancoth, an arrow of gold heading far into the west.

'Grub's up!' called a cheerful voice.

Their Prince was standing behind them, wrapped in the too-big apron, with his sleeves rolled above his elbows. The light of the sunset was in his face, bathing the walls beyond him in gold. And he was offering them golden cider and new-baked bread and a meal better than any they had ever tasted before.